Best Laid Plans
& Other
DISASTERS

Best Laid Plans
& Other
DISASTERS

Amy Rivers

WPP

WOODEN PANTS PUBLISHING

Printed in the United States of America
First Printing, 2017
Wooden Pants Publishing

Cover image used under license from shutterstock.com

ISBN-13: 978-0-692-81780-3

Acknowledgements

To the folks at Wooden Pants Publishing: thank you, Rich Keller, for seeing the potential in Val and Gwen's story and bringing us into your world. And to Jen Schafer for making these books look amazing! Couldn't have done it without you two.

A big shout out to Rachel Weaver at Sandstone Editing. Your thoughtful comments and attention to detail were so critical in getting this book ready for the world.

To the WWTBAW, my writing tribe: Laura, Sarah, Sheala, Joe, David and Ronda with no H. You've given me strength and encouragement through this whole crazy process. You've made me a better writer and a much more critical reader. Thank you for sharing your brilliant work with me and for spending so much time whipping mine into shape!

An extra special boisterous woot woot for Laura Mahal for all your love and support. Thank you for continuing to take my calls, even when I'm so whiny I can barely stand listening to myself. You've rescued me on more than one occasion and inspired me every day since we met.

This book is in great shape due to the hard work and dedication of my beta readers: my mother-in-law Betty, Rachel, Tara, Sarah, Sheala, Laura, Joe, David and Ronda. Thank you for loving my characters even when they're being bratty.

Thank you to Christine Berg, the current mayor of Lafayette, Colorado. It was so great to sit down and talk politics and motherhood with you. I appreciate your candor more than I can say. I'm glad you were willing to talk some sense into Gwen, and, as a woman and a mother, I am grateful for your contributions to the community.

Thank you so much to all my friends who've encouraged me and listened to me drone on and on about my characters and the day-to-day operations of my writing life. To Jessica, for believing that freezing a fish will make it come back to life and for making my life brighter. To Crissy, for delicious visions of book-themed cupcakes. And, to Tara, for loving Gwen so enthusiastically that she got her own book!

A big THANK YOU to my cousin Rachel, who has been my cheerleader since I started this writing journey. There's no one I'd rather explore graveyards with than you!

Mom, Dad, and the best sister a girl could ever ask for, Cam, I love you! Thank you for supporting me, no matter what.

Thank you isn't quite strong enough a sentiment for my husband, Allen, who tells me to keep writing every time I threaten to get a day job. I'm grateful for your insights, your editing skills, your patience and your love. I'm humbled that you've decided to take this crazy journey with me.

And last, but certainly not least, thank you to my sweeties, Isaac and Lily, for thinking it's cool to have a mom who writes. You're the center of my universe and I love you to the moon and back.

CHAPTER ONE

Gwen Marsh nibbled a carrot stick without much enthusiasm and listened with increasing tension as her cousin, Val Shakely, went over the latest developments. Val was getting married in a few short months and was predictably single-minded. Gwen curled up in her chair as a cool breeze on the bistro's patio hinted the approach of fall.

She had trouble following the conversation. Her thoughts were miles away going over the previous night's argument with Jason and the impasse they'd reached before retiring to their respective corners. She knew they couldn't put off talking forever, but she tried to put her worries aside and turn her attention back to Val.

"I don't know why this has to be so complicated!" Val's eyelid twitched as she spoke, and Gwen stifled a laugh. "I suggest every day that we elope, and John just smiles because he knows there's no way I'd let Anne down like that."

Gwen knew Val saw her soon-to-be mother-in-law, Anne Hatfield, as nearly godlike. Gwen couldn't help but smile at Val's exasperation.

"That's what you get for marrying a society man." Gwen took her cousin's hand across the table and gave it a squeeze. "You know it's going to be fine. Anne's doing most of the planning, and at the end of the day, you and John will get to go home and reclaim your quiet lives. It's only one day."

"I know." Val picked up a forkful of salad but put it down before it made it to her mouth. "You know, this wedding is doing wonders for my figure. I'm not even hungry anymore." She pushed her hardly touched plate away from her.

Gwen chuckled. "Yeah, you should have done this a long time ago."

"Hey!"

"That's my feisty girl," Gwen teased. "Listen, I hate to leave you in the middle of your daily wedding crisis, but I've got a meeting at one." She started gathering her purse and coat.

"Off to save the world, Mayor Marsh?" Val asked with a twinkle in her eye. Gwen spent several days each week mentoring teens and working on youth engagement initiatives in the community. She was the first woman mayor of Cambria, as well as the youngest, and she was determined to get more young people involved in politics. Val's expression turned serious. "Wait. Before you go. Any news?"

Gwen had hoped to escape before having to talk about her own relationship issues. She should have known better. Val was no more likely to let the moment pass than Gwen had the tables been turned. That wasn't the way their relationship worked.

"Nothing to report. Things are fine, as usual." Gwen's naturally cheerful demeanor disappeared, replaced by agitation, a feeling that was more common in recent days. Gwen and Jason had dated almost long as John and Val, but where Val's relationship was intense and fast-paced, Gwen's seemed to be in a holding pattern.

As if on cue, Gwen's phone buzzed. There was a text from Jason.

Hey, babe. I need to talk to you.

Gwen sighed, and wondered why Jason never got to the point in texts. Then she chided herself for being so short tempered where he was concerned

Later. I've got a meeting.

2

Gwen felt a twinge of guilt at her dismissive response, but the feeling passed when she saw his response.

Today. This problem isn't going to go away. I have news.

Gwen switched off her phone and threw it in her purse more aggressively than she intended. When she looked up, she realized Val had been watching her text exchange intently.

"Hmm." Val's expression turned dark and cloudy with concern, though that didn't keep her from returning to her earlier line of questioning. "What're you guys waiting for?"

Gwen flinched. She'd heard this question a lot lately. It never failed to make her angry.

"We can't all have the fairytale, Val. Besides, if anything interesting happened in my life, who'd be here to listen to all your wedding worries?"

"Ouch. Okay, I'm sorry I asked."

Gwen felt another pang of guilt. Val was her best friend, besides being her cousin, and her intentions were good. Gwen's temper flared more often lately, and talking about Val's upcoming nuptials seemed to bring out the worst in her.

"I'm sorry, Val." Gwen looked her cousin in the eye. "I don't know what's wrong with me. Jason and I are great together. I don't know why I can't be happy. Sometimes I wonder if I'm cursed to be just like my parents."

Val came around the table and gave Gwen a hug. "This relationship stuff has never come easy for either of us, but we're still in charge of how our lives turn out, no matter what our parents did or didn't do." Val rested her head on Gwen's shoulder. "Your parents are fools, Gwen. I'd never make it through *my* life without you. We're both going to be okay. We just need to hang in here."

Gwen hugged her cousin back but didn't feel reassured. "I've got to run. I'll see you later." She pushed past the crowd waiting to be seated, and her phone buzzed again.

Today, Gwen. Really important.

Gwen groaned. She tried to get her mind on her upcoming meeting but couldn't concentrate. Instead, she focused on her feet, counting her steps as she hurried down the sidewalk toward City Hall.

CHAPTER TWO

Cambria's administration offices were part of a larger municipal complex housing the police department, superior court and the library. In the middle of the complex sat a small city park. It burst with color during the summer months but was dreary now like Gwen's mood.

Gwen walked through the front doors of City Hall and headed for the heavy wooden door that led to the City Clerk's office. Past the reception desk lay a honeycomb of offices, which housed the city's administrators.

"Morning, Barb." Gwen smiled at the clerk.

"Hey, Gwen. I proofed the proclamation. It's on your desk."

"Thank you, ma'am." Gwen continued down the hall to her office.

As part of the city council, the mayor didn't have a designated office. Instead, the mayor shared the council workspace. Due to the fact that council members all had day jobs elsewhere, Gwen often found herself alone. As she turned the handle, Gwen took a quick peek over her shoulder at the doors on the opposite end of the hall.

It seemed fitting that the city manager's office was located opposite the council workspace, like the two heads of a table. The mayor and council shaped policy for the city, while the city manager oversaw day-to-day government operations and implemented council mandates.

Gwen stepped into the office and shut the door behind her, as the city manager's door began to open. Gwen stood for a moment with her back to her door, letting her relief at a narrow escape wash over her.

There was a knock at the door. Gwen took a deep breath before turning to open the door.

"Ah, Mayor Marsh. So good of you to join us today." City Manager Karen Fredrickson stood at the door sneering. Gwen cringed at the formal and yet patronizing way Karen insisted on addressing her.

I haven't had enough coffee for this, Gwen thought.

"What do you need, Karen? I just got here and I have a meeting in ten minutes."

"The city received an anonymous complaint about improprieties in the mayor's office." Karen's smile was as predatory as a tiger. "Looks like your affair with the finance office hasn't gone unnoticed."

Gwen sighed. "What kind of improprieties?"

"Oh. I'm not sure about the specifics. I handed it off to Human Resources," Karen said, smugly.

"Did someone call in?"

"Listen, Mayor Marsh. Some of us have work to do today. If you want more information, you should contact HR. I'm sure they'll want to talk to you." Karen turned, a sly grin on her face, and walked back to her office.

During her years as a councilwoman, Gwen and Karen had gotten along swimmingly. They had formed a bond over their roles as the only two women in positions of power in the city. Having worked closely together, they'd found ways to compromise even when they disagreed, which was fairly often.

But that all changed the minute Gwen was elected as mayor. The camaraderie they'd once shared evaporated like water on a hot sidewalk. Intellectually, Gwen understood some of Karen's reservations. The term of a city manager was often short and big changes in council members could have an immediate impact on the manager's job stability. And Gwen had big plans for Cambria, many of which Karen seemed to think were unrealistic. But that didn't explain the totality of Karen's new antagonistic stance.

Gwen was lost in her thoughts when she heard the door open. She glanced over her shoulder and saw Councilman Deets walk across the room, open the filing cabinet, pull out a file folder, and walk out of the room without a word. Gwen sighed, rubbing her upper arms as if warding off a cold draft.

For years, Gwen dreamed of becoming Cambria's mayor. In her fourth year as a councilwoman, she saw the opportunity to run and took it. Now the realities of the job were making her second guess herself. She'd worked so hard to develop good working relationships with her colleagues and the city staff, only to find herself starting from scratch once her term began. *I'm starting in the hole*, Gwen thought, glumly. Her dream of being the youngest female governor in Colorado seemed impossibly far away.

Gwen walked toward a desk at the back of the room. She heard the ticking of the wall clock in the room's suffocating silence. Despite the tension on the council, Gwen still preferred it when someone else was around. The simple sound of another person tapping keys on the computer or shuffling feet under a desk made her feel far less anxious and alone. Pulling her laptop out of her bag, she quickly booted up and played some music to fill the void.

Luckily, Gwen's one o'clock appointment would be short. She was meeting with the leader of a community group that was organizing an event for voter registration. The event would be aimed at getting young voters registered and informed to increase voter turnout. The organization asked Gwen to speak, and she was really excited. It was one of her favorite parts of her job.

She'd been reading over the proclamation when the group

leader, Evan McDaniel, knocked on the office door. Evan was a junior at the university and his enthusiasm was infectious. Gwen loved meeting with him because it always left her feeling energized.

"Hey, Evan!"

"Hello, Mayor Marsh." Gwen smiled at Evan's awkward formality. He worked very hard at be professional, but once they got started, he quickly got too excited about the project for restraint. Gwen ached for the days when she felt that optimistic about politics. At thirty-two, she already felt more cynical than she would have imagined.

"I've got a draft of the proclamation. Can you take a look?" she asked.

Gwen handed over the piece of paper, her finger brushing Evan's hand as he took it. Evan's cheeks colored, and he hastily turned his full focus to the proclamation. *Uh oh*, Gwen thought, realizing there might be more to Evan's awkwardness around her than she'd suspected. And though she resolved herself to be mindful of her behavior around Evan, she couldn't help but feel flattered.

"This looks great," Evan said, his face still slightly colored. He seemed to be avoiding direct eye contact with Gwen.

"Oh, good. I'll get it finalized then for the event. I'm supposed to be there at six?"

"Yes. We're opening the doors at 5:30. Just after classes let out. We'll have you speak at 6:00, followed by the governor. Is fifteen minutes enough?"

"It's perfect. I'm glad you got him down here." Governor Carlton had been a critical supporter of Gwen in the election, and she admired the work he did, especially related to violence prevention.

"It's going to be great!" Evan's enthusiasm began to chip away at his earlier embarrassment. Gwen was relieved. They talked for a few more minutes before Evan left.

Alone again in the office, Gwen turned the music back up and opened up a report she'd wrestled with all week. She was proposing a modification to the draft city budget and wanted to triple-check her figures. Beyond the resistance and animosity she'd experienced at the hands of her colleagues, any work she presented was rigorously scrutinized. She finally started to get into a groove when she heard a tentative knock at the door.

"Come in."

Gwen turned around to see Jason peeking around the door.

"Hey, sweetie," he said, quietly.

Gwen scrunched her nose in disapproval. Having Jason in her office always made her feel like she was doing something illicit, even though she knew it was irrational.

"I know, I know. I just wondered if you wanted to double with Val and John for dinner tonight? John called a little while ago."

"I don't know." As if on cue, Gwen yawned. "I'm tired. Can we do it another night?" She wasn't up to a night out with the lovebirds, especially after having already got an earful of wedding news from Val at lunch.

Jason frowned. "This is the third invite we've turned down, Gwen. Is there something going on with you and Val?"

"No. It's been a really long week for me. Anyway, I had lunch with her today."

"I think I'd like to go. Would it be okay if we do our own things tonight?"

"I thought you needed to talk to me."

Jason frowned. "I do. But it's pretty clear you're not up to it. Again."

Gwen felt a spark of irritation flare up. She'd been especially aggravated lately, and she was glad she and Jason didn't live together. They fought enough as it was.

"Obviously it wasn't *that* important."

"You know, Gwen. Just because it isn't about you, doesn't make it less important."

9

Gwen's irritation turned to anger, and it took all her restraint to keep from yelling at Jason. She straightened up in her chair and took two purposeful breaths.

"You know what? It's fine. Just go. Tell them I'm sorry." Gwen turned back to her computer, dismissively. She heard Jason sigh and winced as the door clicked closed behind him.

CHAPTER THREE

When Jason made it out to his car, he was so angry he wanted to yell. Even when she was irritable, Gwen wasn't usually so dismissive. Jason leaned against his car door, breathing in slowly, trying to reclaim some sense of calm.

He wasn't built for this kind of drama. Jason didn't have any sisters. He'd spent his childhood blissfully unaware of issues of the opposite sex. His mom loved sports and the outdoors, which, now that he thought about it, may have been a survival strategy in a house of all boys. Jason rarely dated in high school, never interested in embarking on anything too serious. College wasn't much different.

It didn't hurt that his best friend was such an introvert they spent most of their time avoiding crowds. True, Jason grew up around June Hatfield, but that hadn't really counted. June was John's sister and, honestly, she wasn't much into dating either.

Life for Jason was pretty simple, until he met Gwen. Jason had been attracted to Gwen the very first time he saw her walk into the administration building. He'd hand-delivered an overview about his budget presentation to the council, looking for an opportunity to be near her. There was something intensely poised and confident about her, at least back then, and it didn't hurt that she was the most beautiful woman he'd ever seen.

Jason smiled at the memory, his anger fading into the background. He wasn't actually mad at Gwen, not really. He was frustrated, yes. Confused, definitely. But he was also in love. It wasn't more than a couple of weeks into their relationship that Jason started imagining a future for the two of them. It didn't even scare him. He was absolutely sure of his feelings.

Finally opening the door and getting behind the wheel, Jason was determined not to let Gwen's bad mood spoil his day. He saw things weren't easy for her right now at work, and he knew professionalism was extremely important to her. He decided life was too short to stay mad. His time working at the city would be much shorter.

* * *

Gwen was half asleep on her couch with the television turned up loud when the buzzer rang. At first she wasn't sure what she'd heard, then she realized someone was at the door. She looked at her phone. It was almost midnight. She looked through the peephole and saw Jason standing in the hall, rocking back and forth on the balls of his feet. Holding back a groan, Gwen unlocked the door.

"Hi," Jason said, leaning in to kiss Gwen on the cheek.

"Hey."

Jason frowned at Gwen's lack of enthusiasm, and she felt guilty for not being happy to see him. Unfortunately, the guilt reinforced her irritation. Jason walked past her and plopped down on the couch with a yawn. He stretched his arms above his head and finally looked up at Gwen who stood nearby, her arms folded across her chest.

"What's the matter?"

"I'm tired, Jason." Gwen's body was rigid as she stared down at him, uninviting. "I was sleeping. It was a horrible day, and I just need a good night's sleep."

"Let's go to bed then," Jason said, a hopeful smile on his lips. "Then we can talk in the morning. I have some news."

Gwen's frown deepened. "I thought we were taking the night off." His face fell and again she felt guilt-ridden at being so rude,

12

but not enough to apologize. Her body was heavy with fatigue and she felt queasy.

"You want me to leave?" Jason asked. "I'm already here, Gwen. Let's just get some sleep and we'll both feel better in the morning."

Gwen's frustration advanced to full-blown anger. "It was your idea to do our own things tonight. You didn't even call first, Jason. I could have told you on the phone that I wasn't up for visitors."

"Visitors?" Jason asked, suspiciously.

"Visitor. Singular. You. You know what I mean!" Her voice got louder. "Look, I'm exhausted. Can we not do this right now?"

"Oh, for heaven's sakes." Jason got off the couch with dramatic effort. "I don't know what's going on with you right now, Gwen, but it's getting old. You don't want to hang out with John and Val. You don't want me in your office, and now you're kicking me out of your apartment." Jason hesitated, about to say more but thinking better of it. Instead, he brushed past Gwen, opened the door, and walked out without another word.

Gwen locked the door behind him and went back to the couch, laying her head back on the cushion and staring up at the ceiling. Jason was right. Something was going on with her but she couldn't quite put her finger on it.

Distancing herself from him at work had been a necessary action. Since she'd been elected, Jason got nothing but grief from the city manager and other staff in the finance office. They implied that dating the mayor was a conflict of interest, though Gwen and Jason had done everything they could think of to keep their work relationship above board.

Of course, Gwen should have known that her relationship with Jason would be even more challenging once she took office. She'd always spoken out about ethics and professionalism, and she knew her relationship with Jason blurred the lines. With the new complaint on file, there would be even more scrutiny.

Gwen felt anguished. She loved Jason, despite the mess she'd been making of their relationship lately. But maybe this wasn't the right time to be in a relationship, especially with someone she worked with. Gwen felt the sting of tears in her eyes.

CHAPTER FOUR

Gwen was sluggish getting ready for work the next day. In addition to her responsibilities as mayor, Gwen worked as a non-profit management consultant for several organizations. Her background in public administration made her a desirable consultant, and the flexibility of the job made it an ideal source of income while she pursued her political endeavors. But it wasn't always terribly exciting work, and with her stress at its current level, she found it harder to stay motivated.

The life of a management consultant was usually filled with travel, but Gwen's current clients were all located in the Denver area, making travel much easier. If she ever needed to go back to full-time consulting, she'd have to search outside her geographic area for work, but her time on the city council and now as the mayor had her convinced that public service was her calling. Her consulting work paid the bills, but her heart belonged to politics.

Most days, Gwen worked from home, but today she had an afternoon meeting in Denver with one of her clients. She got dressed in a navy pant suit and accessorized with a big silver dolphin pendant Val had gotten for her birthday a few years back. She loved wearing something playful when she dressed for business. It reminded her that even serious things could be fun.

Gwen almost reached the freeway entrance when she realized she'd left the cable from her cell phone car charger at City Hall.

A quick glance at her phone let her know her battery would be dead before she made it back to her house, so she altered her course and headed for the municipal complex. Gwen parked in the two-hour visitor parking lot closest to the building. Her plan was to run in, grab the cable, and be back at her car in less than five minutes. She wanted to get into Denver early and grab some coffee before the meeting.

When Gwen walked into the council office, she was startled to find Karen Fredrickson hunched over her workstation, rifling through some of Gwen's papers. Intent in her search, Karen hadn't heard Gwen enter the room.

"What are you doing here?" Gwen asked. Karen jumped and turned around with a guilty look on her face, which she quickly replaced with a scowl.

"I could ask you the same question," Karen said, keeping her eyes connected with Gwen's in a show of dominance. "You're not on the schedule today."

Gwen walked across the room, pushed Karen aside with her arm, and reached down to the stack of papers the manager had been sifting through.

"These came out of my filing cabinet," Gwen said, turning to see the other woman's reaction. Karen kept her face expressionless, but Gwen noticed she tapped her fingers nervously on her leg.

"I was looking for the recent budget notes," Karen replied, though her eyes gave away the lie.

"If there's something you need from my files, you can contact me." Gwen put the papers back in the cabinet and locked it. "You have no business being in here."

Karen bristled. "I'm the city manager. Everything that happens in this building is my business." The other woman's posture reflected a self-importance that immediately engaged Gwen's defenses. After all, they were all supposed to be on the same team.

"Come on, Karen. You know that's not true." Gwen's temper flared and she worked hard to maintain her restraint. Karen's cheeks began to color. *At least she has the good grace to be embarrassed*, thought Gwen.

"I'll need those notes on my desk first thing tomorrow," Karen ordered, though she knew the words were empty. As city manager, Karen Fredrickson held more power over general operations than did the mayor, but her authority did not give her blanket access to the work of the council.

"Look, Karen. I know you're not thrilled I'm here, though quite honestly I can't begin to understand why." Gwen paused for dramatic effect. "But I suggest you go through proper channels if you want council paperwork. I'd hate to have to file an ethics complaint."

Karen blanched. Gwen was not the type to make threats but there was something very suspicious about Karen's behavior, and it made Gwen feel very uneasy. She wasn't going to let the woman's animosity toward her undermine her work or her authority.

Karen walked out the door without another word, reminding Gwen of Jason's departure the night before. *I certainly know how to clear a room.* She found her charger cable in her desk drawer, right where she'd left it. But before leaving the office, she checked the rest of the filing cabinets, making sure they were locked. Distracted by her run in with Karen, Gwen realized she was now going to be cutting her arrival in Denver close. She headed out to her car, hoping the meeting would go smoothly since she'd be doing it without a much-needed dose of caffeine.

* * *

On the drive home, Gwen got a text from Jason asking her to have dinner with him. They agreed to meet at six so Gwen would have time to change her clothes. Gwen was pretty sure they were going to have a fight. After last night, she was sure Jason wasn't her biggest fan. The thought made her sad. When she let herself relax, she enjoyed his company very much. She was pretty sure the stress of being mayor while simultaneously working on a new relationship was getting to her.

When Gwen walked into the restaurant, she spotted Jason immediately. He was reading something on his phone but he looked up and made eye contact. He did not smile.

Her steps were slow and measured as she approached the table and took a seat. Jason was usually a very easy-going person. Gwen couldn't remember a time when he hadn't greeted her with a smile and a kiss. Now his jaw was set and he fixed his eyes on her with a stare that made her shiver. She prepared herself for the worst.

"Hey," he said, reluctantly. Jason sat rigid in his chair. It looked uncomfortable and didn't suit his personality. Gwen's stomach turned, knowing she was the reason for this unusual demeanor.

"Hey." For a few moments, silence hung between them like an impenetrable fog.

"How was your day?" Jason's shoulders slumped forward. His tone lost some of its intensity and his face relaxed a bit.

"It was okay," Gwen said, not feeling comfortable enough to elaborate. She wanted to tell him about her interaction with Karen but she sensed this was not the time to talk shop. "How was yours?"

"Pretty good, actually." He hesitated before continuing. "I need to talk to you about something."

Gwen's stomach clenched and she realized she was bracing herself for a break-up. "Okay."

"I'm quitting my job."

"Wait. What?"

"I applied for a job with BGB Pharmaceuticals, and I got it." He shifted in his seat, probably in response to the look of utter shock on Gwen's face. It took her a minute to find the right words.

"When did you apply for the job?"

"About two months ago. After that investigation in my office,

I figured out that being with the city wasn't going to work out anymore." Jason's section had been subjected to an audit on suspicion of fraud. The whole group was cleared, but Jason and Gwen had both suspected the tip-off had come from someone in the city who didn't like Jason. Maybe even someone trying to get back at her.

"Why didn't you tell me?" she asked bluntly, the hurt coming through loud and clear in her voice.

Jason studied her face for a moment before answering. "I've been trying to tell you for days. You haven't exactly been approachable."

Gwen felt flushed. She wanted to be angry, to argue with him, but she knew he was right. Something was definitely off between them, and Gwen was pretty sure she was to blame.

"So, when do you start?"

"Monday. I fly out to Chicago for training for a week. Then, I'll be conducting audits on-site at the regional facilities, so I'll be traveling a lot. There might even be some international travel." Jason's eyes brightened, and Gwen could tell he was trying to suppress his excitement.

"That's great," she said, trying to muster some enthusiasm, but her tone was too flat to be believable.

"Gee, thanks, Gwen," Jason said, grumpily. "The least you could do is be happy for me given how horrible you've treated me lately."

Again, Gwen wanted to argue, but the truth in his words kept her silent. She felt too sad. Jason traveling a lot meant less time to spend together. Maybe that's why he'd chosen this job. She'd been so hard to be around lately. Maybe this was his way of breaking things off gently.

"I am happy for you, Jason," she said, then added, "But I'm sad for us."

Jason's expression softened. "I know how you feel. I wasn't sure whether I'd be willing to take this job when I applied, but things have gotten so bad at work I figured I'd better not limit my options." He sighed. "The last few weeks, I keep thinking you're going to break up with me anyway."

Gwen raised her eyebrows. Jason wasn't usually so forth-coming with his feelings, especially when he was scared or stressed out. She realized how much courage it took for him to open up, and all at once she knew with complete certainty she didn't want to break up.

"Listen. I'm sorry I've been so out of sorts lately. Things haven't exactly been going the way I planned, and the tension at work can get pretty unbearable. Maybe you having a new job will help. At least they won't be able to hold that against us anymore." Gwen offered a smile.

Jason considered her for a moment and then smiled back. "It can't be much worse than it's been lately, eh?"

Gwen and Jason spent the rest of the evening talking animatedly about things they hadn't discussed in a while: traveling, family, plans for the holidays. It was like old times, and Gwen felt truly relaxed for the first time in weeks. But the feeling didn't last. Later that night, Gwen lay in bed listening to Jason's soft breathing. She should have felt calm, settled even. Instead, she felt cold dread; not the sort of feelings she wanted when sleeping next to the man she loved. *What's wrong with me?*

CHAPTER FIVE

Jason got out of bed before the sun was up. He dressed quietly, hoping not to wake Gwen, who'd slept in fits and starts. Not sure whether he wanted her to get more rest or that he didn't want to have to deal with her this morning, he made his way out of her apartment like a burglar. The click of the door behind him left Jason feeling relieved, and then monstrously guilty. That was the way things were going these days. It was hard to be around Gwen right now. But when he avoided her, he felt ashamed of himself. Gwen was clearly going through something and his inability to help her made him feel impotent.

Back at his apartment, Jason started a pot of coffee and took a hot shower, anticipating the caffeine waiting for him as he inhaled the rich aroma of his Colombian roast. Jason's mind drifted to Gwen, as it so often did. Gwen was more of a tea drinker. She constantly gave Jason a hard time about his love of coffee. Despite his best efforts to educate her on the wonders of his favorite caffeinated beverage, Gwen still drank Folger's, if she drank coffee at all. Of course, in the beginning, Jason found her lack of coffee knowledge charming. These days he held anything and everything against Gwen.

In the past few weeks, Jason had been steeling himself for the break up, which seemed inevitable. Gwen was distracted and moody. In the year they'd been dating, Jason had never known Gwen to avoid Val. Jason finally went without her. Val tried to hide her concern for her cousin, but Jason felt her anxiety, which caused his frustration with Gwen to increase.

It was still very early when Jason left his apartment and headed for City Hall. Gwen would be coming in today, and he didn't want to run into her. Today would be hard enough. Jason applied for and accepted the job with BGB Pharmaceuticals without a hint of his intentions to his boss, and he wasn't planning on giving much notice, despite feelings of guilt.

Tom Lowry, the head of Cambria's finance department, was the only reason Jason lasted this long after the election. Tom created a barrier between Jason and the office politics. After the ethics investigation, Tom had put himself on the line for Jason, making the working environment almost tolerable.

The problem was Karen Fredrickson. Karen and Jason never had a single issue until Gwen won the election. Now, Karen was out for blood. She couldn't go directly after Gwen, or at least not without raising too many eyebrows, so she did the next best thing by making Jason's work life a living hell.

Jason knew Gwen was going through similar issues with Karen. Luckily, the mayor was part of the larger council, and so Gwen was insulated to some extent. Jason was an easier target. Dealing with city finances put the employees in his department under increased scrutiny, undergoing regular audits and quality control to protect against malfeasance.

Jason had been up front with Tom about his relationship with Gwen, so after the election Tom modified Jason's job to ensure no conflict of interest existed. But that didn't stop someone from reporting an alleged impropriety and triggering a full investigation. The allegations singled Jason out, and it was common understanding in the department that someone was out to get him.

After the matter was cleared up, things didn't go back to normal. Now Jason's co-workers were very guarded around him. He'd had an easy relationship with his colleagues, going to lunch and meeting up after work from time to time. Now the invitations did not come, and Jason's job became very taxing. For the first time since he started with the city, he dreaded going to work.

Dealing with Gwen made it so much worse. Ever since the trouble began with his job, Gwen insisted their already professional distance in the office be even stricter. She especially hated it when he dropped by unannounced. She attempted to never be alone with him at City Hall if she could avoid it, and between this enforced distance and snubbing from his co-workers, Jason was miserable.

* * *

Jason entered City Hall and walked down the hallway toward his department. Most of the employees worked out of cubicles, but Jason had worked his way into a management position and a small office next to Tom's.

Tom was often in the office early, and this morning was no exception. Jason knocked on the door frame to get his boss' attention.

"Jason? You're here early." Tom put down his pen and stood to shake Jason's hand.

"Morning, Tom," Jason said, noting his boss's raised brows. "I've got some news and I hoped to catch you before everyone else got here."

"Okay, shoot."

"I know this is sudden, but I've decided to leave the city. BGB has offered me a senior auditor position and with things the way they are here, I think it's time for me to be somewhere else." Jason could tell from Tom's expression that the news didn't come as a shock.

"I can't say I'm entirely surprised," Tom said, confirming Jason's impressions. "I'm really sorry to lose you, Jason. You've been a real asset to the city, whether they know it or not."

Jason took a breath, and stretched his neck from side to side.

He'd been carrying a lot of tension there and the relief at Tom's reaction was welcome. "Listen, Tom, I appreciate everything you've done for me. Really. These last few months have been stressful, and I wanted you to know how much your support has meant to me."

Tom was about to speak when there was a knock on the door. Jason turned just in time to see the smirk on Karen's face before she reined in her expression.

"Sorry to interrupt, Tom," Karen said, though her tone said otherwise.

"No problem, Karen. What can I do for you?"

"I need to see your budget notes. I've noticed some discrepancies with what the council gave me, and I want to make sure I have the most recent versions so I can double check."

The tension was back in Jason's neck in response to Karen's tone. Most of the time, the council and the city staff worked well together, especially on the city budget. But with Gwen as the mayor, it seemed like Karen was on the lookout for any way to discredit the council and, more specifically, their leader. Karen and Gwen had gotten along while Gwen was a council member, and Jason suspected the growing hostility was a result of Karen's insecurity about Gwen's dramatic success in the election.

"Sure. I'll send a copy over in a few minutes, after I finish up with Jason."

Karen frowned. "Okay. But I need it as soon as possible. I'm sure whatever Jason needs can wait a while, can't it?" She looked right at Jason, her glare raising goosebumps on his arms while simultaneously causing his face to flush.

Jason cleared this throat. "Actually, I'm done here." He handed Tom his official letter of resignation. "Again, I'm sorry for the short notice, Tom." Then, turning to Karen, he added, "I'm sure it'll be good to get some new blood in here." He walked past Karen toward his office, brushing her arm as he passed her. He heard her asking Tom for clarification as soon as he was out of sight, and he was quite sure the news of his departure would spread quickly.

With only two days left in his job at the city, Jason started tying up loose ends and transferring projects to his colleagues. Since Jason had been relieved of any solo projects after Gwen became mayor, it wasn't hard to redistribute his work. By the end of Friday, Jason had made his peace with his decision to take the new job and was even looking forward to it.

At 4:59, Jason turned off his computer, put on his coat, and picked up a small box of his personal effects, leaving his office empty and sterile. He felt eyes on him as he made his way to the door. Outside the finance office, Jason saw Karen loitering near the entrance to the city Clerk's office, a look of satisfaction etched on her face. For a moment, Jason felt a twinge of frustration at having let Karen win. But with every step toward the door, the feeling dissipated.

As he walked out of City Hall for the last time, Jason thought, *goodbye and good riddance.*

CHAPTER SIX

Gwen had been at Jason's apartment all morning Saturday under the guise of helping him pack, but the truth was more desperate. For some time, Gwen distracted herself from everyone, Jason included. But now that Jason was leaving, even though it was only for a week, Gwen's insecurity and uneasiness reached a peak, her manic energy radiating off her in waves. She'd been underfoot as Jason packed because she couldn't bring herself to leave him, fearing she'd never see him again despite his reassurances.

"How about this one?" she asked, holding up a long-sleeved cream shirt.

"I'm good," Jason said, not looking up. She could tell from his tone that his patience was barely in check. Gwen cringed.

"Do you need me to grab you a plastic bag for your toiletries?"

"No, I've got it." Jason closed his suitcase and turned to face Gwen. "Listen, babe. I'm pretty much done here. I need to go do some laundry and get the apartment ready."

Gwen's stomach churned and she rubbed her belly trying to relieve her discomfort. "I'm just trying to help."

"I know. But I don't really need anything and it looks like you need some rest." He looked concerned, but he didn't make a move toward her. They'd been snapping at each other earlier and he seemed content to make her feel awkward about sticking around without explicitly telling her to go.

Taking the hint, Gwen made her way back to her own apartment, but only after Jason swore he'd be over to her place early in the evening. Gwen turned on the television and sat on her couch, barely moving for almost an hour, disgusted with the sudden onset of neediness. Her stomach rolled, and she finally got up to make some toast, reluctantly giving in to the growling in her abdomen. Her increasing anxiety kept her appetite at bay, but if she went too long without eating, she started feeling queasy. The nausea was bad enough that, by the end of the week, she finally scheduled a checkup with her doctor for the following week.

Gwen had settled back onto her couch and started to wonder what the heck she was watching when the phone rang, causing her to jump.

"Hello?"

"Hey, Gwen." Val's voice sounded tired, but Gwen felt comforted by it. She and Val usually found a way to get together at least every few days, but for the past month Gwen had been avoiding even these social situations. She realized she missed her cousin.

"Hi, Val. What's going on?"

"Wondered how you were doing today. John got off the phone with Jason a few minutes ago, and he seemed concerned."

Gwen felt her irritation flare up. It was one thing to feel appalled by her own feelings of loneliness and insecurity. It was quite another for her friends to be talking about it behind her back. "I'm fine."

After a brief pause, Val continued. "I wanted to see if you'd meet me for lunch on Monday. I talked to my mom last night and wanted to go over a few wedding things with you."

Gwen sighed. Another lunch talking about Val's fabulous society wedding. Her mind grappled for a plausible excuse.

Val added, "I promise I'll keep the wedding talk to a minimum."

A wave of guilt washed over Gwen. She'd found it harder to disguise her boredom with the wedding planning and Val was catching on. Gwen wasn't sure why she felt so annoyed at the prospect of helping. She wished her cousin nothing but happiness. Heck, she'd practically pushed her into the relationship with John, kicking and screaming.

"Sure. Can we do soup and salad?" Gwen asked.

Val and Gwen had a favorite spot for this kind of meal. The salad bar was extensive and Gwen was almost sure she'd be able to stomach some soup, if nothing else.

"Stomach still giving you trouble?" Val asked, her voice riddled with concern for her usually vital cousin. "Wouldn't it be funny if you were pregnant," Val teased, though the concern was still there.

"Don't even joke." Gwen chuckled. "Thank goodness for birth control. Anyway, I made an appointment for Tuesday. I don't know what's going on. It's probably stress but I'm down to toast as my most reliable food source. It sucks."

"Do you want me to go with you since Jason will be out of town?" Gwen cringed a little at the reminder.

"Nah, it's a routine check-up. He'll probably tell me I have an ulcer. With the way I've been feeling, it wouldn't surprise me." Gwen found herself slipping into comfortable conversation with Val. To her relief, it felt almost normal.

"Okay. We'll do a light lunch on Monday and I'll try and distract you." The tone of Val's voice brightened noticeably.

Gwen tried to fight off her annoyance, though she could almost hear the wedding bells ringing in Val's head.

"Sounds good. Jason'll be here in a few hours. I think I'm going to try to take a nap."

"Okay. Get some rest. And Gwen ... I love you, honey."

"Love you, too," Gwen said, surprised to feel tears forming in her eyes. She'd been a horrible friend to Val lately and the sentiment made her emotional. Setting the alarm on her phone,

Gwen lay down on the couch and closed her wet eyes. She was asleep in no time.

* * *

Gwen woke up from her nap feeling refreshed and even a little hungry. Jason knocked at her door a little after five o'clock and she welcomed him with a warm hug. She felt his tension release as they embraced and, for a moment, she was "in love" just like the good old days.

"Want to grab a bite?" Jason asked, pulling away a few inches to see her face.

"We could do that. I actually feel kind of hungry."

"How about the diner?" Jason asked, referring to one of their favorite neighborhood haunts.

Gwen nodded and grabbed her purse from the kitchen table. They walked hand in hand toward the local shopping center. The air was crisp as autumn took hold of Cambria. She shivered, thinking she should have brought a jacket. But when they arrived at the diner, she was met with a blast of warm air that made her stomach roll, and she was immediately glad she hadn't overdressed.

They took a booth near the restrooms. Gwen ordered a Sprite hoping to settle her stomach enough to eat a decent meal. The image of her favorite cheeseburger, dripping with mustard and stacked high with pickles and tomatoes, made Gwen's mouth water, but she decided on a turkey sandwich to play it safe.

"Are you all packed?"

Jason had been staring out the window and her words took him by surprise. Jerking his neck around, he said, "What? Oh … yeah. And I cleaned out the refrigerator so I'll have to shop again when I get back next week."

"That's good." The conversation stalled and Jason turned his attention back to the window and the street beyond.

A few minutes later, the food was delivered to their table. The smell of the turkey sandwich had Gwen salivating, but after a couple of bites, her stomach started to protest and even the smell was no longer enticing. She put the sandwich down in favor of more Sprite. Even Jason's burger looked less than appealing.

"You alright?" Jason asked between bites.

"I'm going to take it easy on the eating until after I see the doctor." Gwen and Jason speculated at length about her stomach problems, though lately Jason seemed more frustrated than sympathetic, as if her misbehaving stomach was somehow self-imposed.

Another long pause followed while Jason polished off his burger and Gwen picked at her sandwich. The distance between them felt much greater than the table width. Gwen looked at Jason and wondered how they'd gotten to this point. The deterioration in their relationship seemed so sudden. There had been a lot of added stress when she took the job as mayor, but they'd managed to shoulder it for months. Looking back, Gwen wasn't sure whether her foul mood was the cause or the result of their current trouble.

Finally, she said, "Jason. Can we talk about what's going on here? We've been avoiding the conversation for a while and with you leaving, I'm worried we'll never have it."

Jason stiffened. She knew talking about feelings was not his favorite thing. "I agree. What's going on, Gwen? I feel like things were going so great and now … well, now they're not."

Jason's verbal maneuvering seemed full of blame, though Gwen could tell he painstakingly avoided putting it into words. She fought off the urge to get defensive. She wasn't at all sure her resolve would last long. "I think things have probably gotten worse for me since I've been feeling so sick. But it also doesn't seem like we're getting along very well right now," she said, treading lightly.

Gwen shuddered. The "where is this relationship going" talk was a perilous dance, especially when you didn't want to break up. For weeks, Gwen felt ambivalent about their relationship. But since Jason announced his change in jobs, she felt a strong pull to work things out. The thought of him being gone so much of the time had shocked to her system.

"For me, the hardest thing has been work. It's been super stressful in the department, and then, with you keeping me at arm's length, I've been feeling pretty depressed."

Gwen nodded, encouraging him to continue. *This is actually going better than I thought.* She felt some of the tension leave her body.

"I really think this new job is going to make the whole situation a lot easier on both of us."

Gwen couldn't help but feel a little resentful at the enthusiasm in his voice. "Easier because you won't be here," Gwen pouted. She despised the weakness in her tone but her words were honest enough. She'd been studying her hands when she spoke, but now she looked up and realized how provocative her words had been. Jason's jaw was set, and she saw anger in his eyes.

"You know, this whole relationship isn't only about you, Gwen. I've gone along with a lot of things you insisted we do, like not moving in together and not holding hands anywhere near the office, because it was important to you. It would be nice if you supported me now and the things *I* need."

"I don't seem to recall you putting up much of a fight about moving in together," Gwen fumed. The relief she'd felt earlier was completely gone, replaced by an anger and hurt that seemed entirely disproportionate to their argument.

"You didn't leave me much choice, Gwen. You made it clear we'd be doing things your way."

Gwen flinched as if she'd been stabbed with a burning hot skewer. "I'm sorry I've been such a pushy bitch!" The moment the words were out of her mouth, Gwen realized they were causing a scene. The conversation in the booths around them quieted and several sets of eyes were focused on her.

Jason's face was red, his shoulders tight with tension, when

Gwen said, through gritted teeth, "Maybe we should continue this conversation at home."

When Jason spoke, his voice was low and angry. "That's right, Gwen. We wouldn't want anyone to talk about the personal life of Mayor Marsh." Even as he said the words, the venom in his voice died down, but the words still hit their mark. Tears sprang to Gwen's eyes and she couldn't control them.

She dashed to the restroom and locked herself into a stall, sobbing silently and wiping at her eyes with handfuls of toilet paper. She heard the door open and close several times, but she stayed as still as possible, hoping if she remained there long enough, everyone out in the dining room would have lost interest.

Have I really been that unreasonable? Sure, she'd insisted on a professional distance at work, but when they'd talked about moving in together, hadn't she made a good argument for waiting? She couldn't remember now. At the time, it seemed like a non-issue. Only in the last few weeks, when she'd begun feeling jealous of Val's wedding planning, had she started to wonder why her relationship with Jason seemed to be slowing down. She'd been waiting for him to move things forward, but hadn't he tried? Had she misconstrued the situation? Was it really fair for her to have put all the responsibility of this ailing relationship on Jason?

Though Gwen felt thoroughly sad, her tears dried up, and after a few minutes she made her way back out into the dining room. Jason paid the bill and, without a word, they walked out of the diner and back to Gwen's apartment. Jason didn't offer to stay the night, as his flight left early the next morning, and Gwen, still feeling weak and wounded, didn't ask.

CHAPTER SEVEN

Jason's flight to Chicago was delayed, and by the time he reached his hotel, he was exhausted. He spent the rest of the day dozing. Waking up the following morning, he felt refreshed for the first time in ages. Whether it was the distance from his life in Cambria or the view of the Chicago skyline out his hotel window, the sun peeking up around a nearby skyscraper, Jason felt ready to take on the world.

An early riser, Jason started his morning in the hotel's exercise room. Then, after showering and dressing for his first day of training, he headed downtown and found a quaint little bistro a block away from BGB headquarters. He ordered a delicious smelling breakfast sandwich on a fresh, buttery croissant. Jason savored every bite and then walked cheerfully to the BGB building.

It was a beautiful day in Chicago. Cold but sunny, and the wind hadn't picked up yet. Unable to resist the aroma of coffee when he entered the building, Jason grabbed a cup from the shop in the lobby before heading upstairs. Training was held in a conference room on the twenty-third floor of the BGB tower with stunning views of the city and Lake Michigan in the distance. Jason was the first to arrive. He stood by the window, admiring the calm waters of the lake, when he heard the conference room door open behind him.

Two men and a woman walked in and laid their things down

on the table. The men appeared to know each other. The woman adjusted the hem of her skirt compulsively. Her dark brown hair was pulled up into an elegant chignon, and her expensive look-ing skirt suit gave an impression of confidence that didn't match the expression on her face. She looked up from the table and caught Jason staring at her.

"Hi," she said, shyly, a small smile turning up the corners of her mouth.

"Hi." Jason walked over to offer his hand. "I'm Jason Turri. I'm training for the Western Division Senior Auditor position."

The woman's smile grew wider, finally making its way to her eyes and Jason found himself inexplicably drawn to her. "Alexandra Barnes," she said, shaking his hand vigor-ously. "I go by Alex. I'm here for the Western Division, too. I'm a project manager."

Jason took the seat next to Alex as the two men finished their conversation. The younger of the two men took a seat across the table, but the older man remained standing.

"Alright, let's get started. Hello, everyone. Welcome to BGB. My name is Daniel Lathan. I'm the CFO of BGB and will be working with each of you in some capacity. The Western Division head, Bill Mackey, will be here in about an hour. I met John here," he paused, indicating the younger man, "at his interview, but I wasn't able to make the other two. My apologies. You must be," he looked down at the sheet in front of him, "Jason." He shook Jason's hand. "And, Alexandra."

"Alex." The CFO shook Alex's hand briefly and then began a rehearsed speech about BGB corporate culture and the expec-tations for all new employees. As he spoke, he passed around large binders containing the employee handbook and other miscellaneous paperwork.

"Inside you'll find non-disclosure agreements which I'll ask you to read and sign now. Then, after training today, you'll need to stop downstairs for your badges."

The next hour flew by in a blur of paperwork, and when the group took a break, Jason's head swam with new information. He got up to stretch and headed to a table in the back of the room for some water. He finished filling his cup as Alex walked up next him.

"Water?" He said, handing her his glass. She nodded and took it, gulping down the glass like she was dying from dehydration.

"Oh, my God, thank you so much." Alex put her glass down on a nearby tray. "I can hardly keep my thoughts straight." Jason could see how overwhelmed she was.

"It's okay. I think we're all feeling that way." With a quick glance back toward the table, he added, "Maybe not John." Their new co-worker leaned back in his chair, his arms stretched behind his neck looking like he was relaxing on a beach rather than attending new employee training.

Jason's words were rewarded with a big smile and a giggle from Alex, and he was surprised to feel himself flush nervously. But there was no time to scrutinize this response. Their direct supervisor, Bill Mackey, walked through the door at that precise moment, and for the next seven hours the group of new employees were inundated with information.

At 4:50, Bill stopped his talk mid-sentence and said, "Okay folks, I think we've done enough for today." He smiled at the glassy eyes that met his. Even John looked disheveled.

"Look, guys, I know this is a lot to take in. But rest assured, everything you need to know is written down somewhere. I've been with BGB for more than a decade, and it's a great company to work with. I promise I won't let you guys drown out there."

Those reassurances did the trick. The group heaved a collective sigh of relief, packed up their briefcases, and staggered out the conference room with three new binders to study. Alex walked ahead of Jason, still in conversation with Bill. By the time the elevator reached the lobby, John and Bill disembarked, and it was just Alex and Jason.

"Want to grab some dinner?" Jason said, feeling a guilty pang as the words left his mouth.

Alex smiled. "Sure. Are you staying at the Sheraton?"

"I am. Guessing they put us all up there."

"Let's share a cab," Alex suggested. "I don't want to carry these binders all the way back to the hotel."

Jason hailed a cab and soon they were entering the hotel lobby.

"Meet back down here at seven?" Alex checked her watch.

"Sounds good."

They rode the elevator together. Alex's room was on the third floor. She gave a nod as she stepped off the elevator and Jason continued his ride up to the ninth floor. As soon as he got to his room, he tossed the binders on one of the beds and flopped down on the other. His brain threatened to explode with all the new facts flurrying around in there, but what caused the most anxiety could be summed up in one word: Alex.

Jason had been away from Cambria one day and he was already crushing on a girl he'd only just met. His thoughts of Gwen were full of anguish. As he lay there, pondering his relationship with Gwen, he wondered whether he should cancel dinner with Alex. But they hadn't exchanged numbers so he'd at least have to meet her downstairs. Sighing, Jason got up and changed into some casual clothes. With half an hour till he was supposed to meet Alex, he'd settled down to watch a few minutes of the local news when his hotel phone rang.

"Hello?"

"Hey." Gwen's voice made Jason's stomach do a little flip. Despite the hard times they'd been having, the sound of her voice always made his heart thump a little faster.

"Wait. Why are you calling me on the hotel phone?" he asked, searching the room for his cell phone, which wasn't visible.

"Your cell is off."

"Must not have turned it back on after training. My brain was pretty dead at that point."

"Long day?"

"Extremely. But everyone is really helpful and supportive so it's not too bad. My co-workers seem really nice. A lot of information to digest though."

"That's good," said Gwen, but her voice sounded strained. "How're you?"

"I'm okay. My stomach has gone from perpetually queasy to painful, but my appointment is tomorrow, so hopefully I can figure this out." Jason could tell from her voice that Gwen felt worse than she let on.

"Are you going to be okay tonight?"

"Val is on-call in case I need her. I'm going to take some Pepto Bismol and go to bed early."

Jason was worried. "Man, I'm sorry I'm not there, babe. Maybe I should come home?" Even though they'd been fighting for weeks, something about Gwen needing him gave Jason a sense of purpose.

"No, I'll be alright. Text you tomorrow and let you know what the doctor says." Gwen's voice turned hard. Jason wasn't sure if it was the pain talking or if he'd said something wrong. He was about to ask her what was up when she said, "I'm going to go lie down. Love you."

"Love you, too" Jason said, wincing a bit at the click that followed immediately. Something was definitely off with Gwen, but she'd been so hard to deal with that Jason relieved he was out of the middle of it this week. He hoped Gwen found some physical relief and, even more importantly, that feeling better would improve her mood.

Ten minutes later, Jason made his way to the lobby to meet Alex.

* * *

After such a long day, Alex and Jason agreed the hotel restaurant would be ideal for dinner. Neither of them wanted to trudge around Chicago. The wind picked up causing the temperature to plummet.

The host led them to a table near the back of the restaurant. They took a seat, ordered wine, and studied their menus with rapt attention. Jason began arranging his silverware, a nervous habit. He was still worried about Gwen.

"So, where did you work before BGB?" Alex asked. Jason was relieved to have the silence broken with a neutral topic.

"I live in Cambria. That's in Colorado, outside Denver." Jason felt like he was bumbling along but he pressed on. "I worked in finance for the city."

"Wow," Alex arched her eyebrows, clearly impressed. "Why did you leave?"

Jason relaxed a little bit. He'd been debating how honest he would be about his life in Cambria, but he felt comfortable with Alex. "About a year ago, my girlfriend Gwen was elected mayor, and apparently that didn't settle well with someone. It's been hell ever since. I finally had enough, and the BGB opportunity was too good to pass up." Having gotten Gwen out on the table, Jason felt hugely relieved. He knew he wasn't the kind of guy to step out on his girlfriend, even if she had been rather impossible lately.

"That must've been a hard decision," Alex said, seeming genuinely interested.

"Not really. By the time I left, the environment was so bad that I dreaded going into work. They'd taken away half my responsibilities anyway to avoid conflicts of interest. Honestly, I'm not sure why I stayed as long as I did. I'm looking forward to being useful again." It felt good to get this off his chest. Alex was easy to talk to, and he realized how much he'd needed someone to confide in. "So, what about you?"

"Oh, nothing so intriguing, really. I was a project manager for a cruise line and they downsized. I've always wanted to travel, so I jumped at the opportunity with BGB. I live in Salt Lake City but there's nothing really holding me there. My family is mostly in California."

"What's in Salt Lake?"

Alex's cheeks reddened momentarily. "Nothing, really. I was married, but the divorce was finalized about three years ago. I haven't dated much since then. As it turns out, Salt Lake isn't my kind of town."

"How'd you end up there?" Jason asked. "Is that where your company was based?"

"No. I moved there with my husband. I worked remotely for a company in Seattle. Made a few trips up there every year, but otherwise I spent most of my time at home or in coffee shops. It got old. I wasn't thrilled when I got laid off, but it didn't take long to see that it was a good thing."

"You didn't want to move back to California?"

"Not really. I mean, I love my family and I love the beach," Alex's eyes lit up. "But I wanted to take this opportunity to meet new people and travel while nothing is tying me down. How does your girlfriend feel about you having to travel so much?"

Jason felt a twinge of guilt. Gwen had been so clingy this weekend, very unlike her. Jason really hadn't given her any say in the matter. "I think she'll be okay," he rationalized. "Her work is pretty busy. She does the mayor gig part-time and then runs a consulting business."

"Any pictures?"

Jason felt awkward showing pictures of Gwen to another woman, but he pulled out his cell phone and found a recent image of Gwen grinning with a big bouquet of roses he'd sent her.

"She's beautiful," Alex said, smiling. Jason smiled too, thinking about Gwen again. She was still the most beautiful woman he'd ever seen. He tucked his phone back in his pocket.

The conversation continued on from there. Jason and Alex connected on so many topics. Jason started to ward off yawns and was surprised when a quick glance at his watch revealed the time; almost midnight. He looked around the room and realized they were the only ones left in the restaurant.

"Man, it's late," he complained, taking one last sip of his water. "I don't know about you, but I'm going to have to get some sleep or I'll never make it through another day like today." Jason's smile was sheepish.

Alex grinned. "I'm with you. I'm glad we don't have to be in until nine tomorrow." She stood, yawning. They made their way to the hotel elevator and headed up to their rooms.

After saying goodnight to Alex, Jason went over the night in his head. He'd started out the evening worrying he might be doing something he'd regret. But Alex was so easygoing he'd soon found himself engaged in the conversation without any inappropriate thoughts. As he lay down to bed, he felt happy to have made a new friend and when he thought about Gwen, it was with renewed hope.

CHAPTER EIGHT

Tuesday morning, Gwen woke up feeling a little bit better. She'd slept almost twelve hours and was relieved that the rest appeared to have helped. *More early nights for me,* she thought as she got ready for work. Gwen planned to work on a pressing project first thing, but feeling better made her want to get out of the house. She pulled on a pair of tennis shoes and headed out for a walk around the neighborhood.

After returning to her apartment, invigorated by the sunshine, Gwen found herself humming as she worked. She felt more like herself than she had in weeks. She worked happily for a few hours before lunch with Val. Gwen regretted her plan to meet for soup and salad. She felt ravenous and craved a more substantial meal. She met Val at the entrance to the restaurant.

"Hey!" Val said, giving Gwen a big hug. "You look like you're feeling better."

Gwen winced, realizing what she must have looked like before. "I am. I actually woke up feeling more or less normal this morning. Thinking about canceling my appointment."

"Don't. You need to get checked out, just in case." Val was ever the more practical of the two, and Gwen conceded that one good morning wasn't good enough excuse to ignore a month of illness.

"No worries. But I'm ordering a sandwich with my soup. I'm starving."

Val chuckled. "You *are* feeling better."

The women sat down at a table near the window, basking in the sunlight shining through. Gwen dove into her sandwich, finishing it a few minutes later. Val looked like she was about to comment when her expression darkened. "You okay?"

"I think I ate too fast." Gwen's face skewed with pain.

"You think?" Val grinned, but her face was awash with concern. "Want me to get you some Sprite?"

"Would you?" Gwen asked, her breathing coming in short bursts. Gwen's face was red and beads of sweat were forming on her brow. Val went to get a Sprite and when she returned, Gwen took a few tentative sips. "I'm going to call the doctor and see if I can get in early," she said, picking up her phone.

Gwen fidgeted uncomfortably while she spoke with the nurse. "No. No, I felt fine this morning but I ate lunch, and now I've got this really bad pain in my stomach." She paused, listening. "No, it's more like a really bad cramp but it's closer to my belly button. Yes. Uh huh. Are you sure? Alright." Gwen hung up the phone.

"What did she say?" Val asked, packing up her purse as if expecting to make a mad dash to the doctor's office.

"She said to go to the emergency room. The doctor can't see me early, and she said the amount of pain I'm having may require a more thorough examination." Gwen gritted her teeth as she spoke.

"Okay, let's go then."

"You don't have to …" Gwen started, but Val cut her off.

"Don't be silly. You look like you can hardly straighten up. You shouldn't be driving. My car is across the street. Let's go." Val offered Gwen a hand and wrapped her arm around her cousin's shoulder as they made their way to the car.

Both women were silent on the way to the hospital. Gwen focused her energy on breathing, which seemed more difficult with the constant pain.

Val reached over to feel Gwen's forehead. "Yikes. Kind of

clammy. We're almost there," she said as much to reassure herself as Gwen.

Val pulled into the emergency room visitor parking lot of St. Anthony's. She helped Gwen out of the car and they headed into the building. Val checked Gwen in and brought over the intake forms. As she filled them out, Gwen looked around the waiting room. There were only a few other people waiting. She hoped they'd get in to see the doctor quickly. The antiseptic smells and sterile coloring scheme of the emergency room made her feel more nervous.

"Gwen?" A nurse peeked her head around the corner.

"That was fast," Val muttered as she helped Gwen up, grabbing the intake forms to finish in the room. Gwen felt a little light-headed. Being called back right away gave her the sense that she was in serious trouble.

The nurse took her vitals and asked a long string of questions related to the location and intensity of the pain, how long she'd had it, medications she took, and her stress level. Gwen answered each question through gritted teeth. Finally, the nurse handed her a cup and said, "I need a urine sample, and then we'll get you settled in a room. I'll be able to give you some pain killers to help with the pain."

Gwen nodded her head and walked slowly toward the restroom. Val waited, tapping her foot nervously with each passing minute. Gwen finally emerged, handed off her sample, and the two women followed the nurse to a room near the charge station. The nurse took a hospital gown out of a cabinet and handed it to Gwen.

"Go ahead and change, then lie down. I'll be right back." The nurse hurried out into the hallway, closing the door behind her.

Gwen eased herself out of her clothes and into the gown, allowing Val to tie the back, but still shivering at the garment's draftiness. Then she sank down onto the bed and closed her eyes. Val took a seat to the side.

"How're you feeling?" Val asked her cousin.

"A little better," Gwen said. Her breathing was smoother now that she was lying down. "Exhausted," she said, her eyes still closed.

"I bet," Val said, stroking Gwen's cheek. "Do you want me to call Jason?"

Gwen hesitated. "No, he's in training, and I don't really know *what* to tell him. I don't want to worry him," she said, but she sounded unsure.

"Okay, let me know," Val said, reluctantly.

After about ten minutes, the nurse came back in, handing Gwen a cup with water. "You're not allergic to any medications, right?" Gwen shook her head, and the nurse handed her another cup with two pills in it. "Take these. We're sending in the ultrasound tech. Then the doctor will be in to see you."

Gwen gulped the pills and lay back. "Ultrasound?"

The nurses nodded. "If you've got an ulcer or a cyst, we'll need to see it to determine a course of treatment."

It took another twenty minutes before the ultrasound tech arrived, but luckily the pain medication kicked in, and Gwen started to doze off. The technician appeared to be in her forties. She wore a *My Little Pony* scrub top and her graying hair pulled back in a ponytail.

Gwen opened her eyes. "I love your top!" she said, mustering as much enthusiasm as she could manage.

The tech smiled. "My daughter picked it out for me. She's six." She shuffled around getting her equipment set up. "I'm going to squeeze some of this gel on your stomach. It might be a little cool." She pulled the blanket up to Gwen's abdomen and then raised the gown to gain access to her stomach. The gel was barely lukewarm, and Gwen flinched a bit when it hit her skin, then she relaxed. The tech pulled out her wand and began probing around on Gwen's belly.

"Does this hurt?" she asked, acknowledging Gwen's negative

response and moving on. After a few minutes she said, "All done." She wiped the excess gel off of Gwen's belly and pulled her gown back down. Seeing the look of concern on her face, the tech added, "Don't worry. The doctor will be in soon. I'm sure the baby will be fine."

Val felt the color rise in her cheeks and a quick glance at her cousin revealed a look of shock.

"Wait. What? I don't understand," Gwen said, stammering.

It was the ultrasound tech's turn to look flustered. "You knew you were pregnant?" she asked, though it was clear from her face that she knew the answer.

"No." Gwen said, and though she might have had more to say, no words came out of her mouth. Instead, the blood seemed to have left her face completely.

"I'm sorry. I didn't realize. I shouldn't have said anything." The technician looked worried. "The doctor is going to kill me." Then she smiled at Gwen and said, "Congratulations," as she pulled her cart back out the door.

It took a moment before Gwen's head turned in Val's direction. The two women looked at each for a moment, unable to find the right words. Finally, Val said, "Holy crap."

"How did this happen? I'm on birth control." Gwen's voice was hardly more than a whisper.

They sat in complete silence for a very long time. Eventually, the doctor came in, confirming the technician's revelation.

"I'm going to order a few more tests, but I don't see anything to be worried about. Women's bodies can react in many strange ways to pregnancy. Some women have pain even with normal pregnancies, but I want you to follow up with your doctor soon so we can keep an eye on things. I'm going to give you some painkillers in case you need them, but use them sparingly and don't take any over the counter medicine without consulting your OB/GYN. Obviously, you'll need to discontinue the birth control immediately."

"How did this happen?" Gwen asked almost to herself, her voice still barely audible.

The doctor chuckled. "I'm pretty sure you know how this happened." He paused, giving her hand a squeeze. "Birth control isn't 100% effective. *Accidents happen*. I'd like you to follow up with your OB/GYN today if possible. Since you've had some pain, they'll want to make sure everything stays okay."

Accidents happen. The words rang in Gwen's ears and she fought to regain control over her emotions.

The doctor left the room to sign off on her discharge paperwork. Gwen was quiet for a few more moments, but then she turned to Val with a grin on her face saying, "I guess that explains why I've been such a bitch lately." Despite her attempt at humor, Gwen's eyes glistened, conflicting emotions surging within her.

Val laughed and put an arm around her. Gwen knew there'd be a lot more to say, but for the moment she took comfort in Val's embrace and, for once, enjoyed the silence.

CHAPTER NINE

"Are you sure you want to go?" Val asked a few days later, as she zipped up the back of Gwen's dress. Val spent the majority of her free time since the hospital visit with Gwen, who teetered precariously between relief at knowing what was going on inside her body and abject terror at the implications.

"Of course I'm going," Gwen said, pulling on her blazer. "I've been working on this event for months. The group is counting on me." She paused, taking a deep breath. "Besides, no matter what's going on in my personal life, I still have a responsibility to this community." This last bit seemed to have been added for her own benefit.

"I wish I could come, but I told Anne I'd meet her for dinner."

"It's okay, Val. You've been a lifesaver this week, and a night off of this roller coaster will probably be a relief." Gwen turned to face Val, fighting back tears. "I wish I could go with you." Gwen's sudden show of weakness elicited a look on shock from Val. Gwen was definitely not the one to show fear.

"Jason's home tomorrow, right? Have you figured out how you're going to tell him?" Val paused. "Or even what you're going to tell him?" She and Gwen had gone rounds on this topic for several days, and as far as Val could see, Gwen still hadn't made up her mind. "Gwen?"

Gwen looked down and sighed. "I need a little bit more time to get my brain wrapped around this."

Val put her hands gently on her cousin's shoulders. "I know you're freaking out, Gwen, but you're going to have to tell Jason. And the sooner the better."

"I know," Gwen said, miserably. "It's just that things haven't been going very well between us, and now he's got this new job and he seems so happy. I have no idea how he's going to react."

"Jason loves you. It's going to be okay." Val gave Gwen's shoulder a squeeze. "Listen, I'll be out with Anne until about nine. If you want me to come over after ..."

"That's alright, Val. I'm going to come home and go straight to bed. Go home and spend time with John."

Val nodded, picked up her jacket, and walked toward the front door. "Call me if you need me, okay? Love you."

"Love you, too," Gwen said, fighting back a new wave of tears. She waited until Val was out the door before grabbing a tissue and dabbing at her eyes. She took a few more breaths to regain her composure, grabbed her purse, and headed out the door. She looked forward to the distraction of the event and an opportunity to spend some time as the mayor instead of the train wreck she'd become in the last few days.

* * *

Gwen arrived at the civic center about thirty minutes ahead of schedule. She parked and then walked into the auditorium, looking for Evan. She spotted him working on the audiovisual equipment and headed in his direction.

"Hi, Evan."

She'd intended to say more but Evan was so focused on the task at hand that she'd made him jump.

"I'm so sorry," Gwen said, offering an apologetic hand. "I wanted to check in. I know I'm early."

Recovering, Evan said, "Oh, gosh, no, it's fine. Thank you for coming, Mayor Marsh. I'm working on a few last minute preparations. Can I get you something to drink?"

"A bottle of water would be wonderful, but don't rush. I'm

going to wander around a bit." Gwen left Evan to his work and walked back to the entrance of the auditorium. A series of posters were displayed on easels, describing Cambria's voter registration and turnout statistics from the past few years in comparison with the state of Colorado as a whole. Whoever put them together did a great job.

Before long, people started drifting through the front doors. Several people recognized Gwen, and soon she was in her element, shaking hands and engaging in conversation with her constituents. This was the part of the job that Gwen loved.

"Mayor?" Evan approached with a bottle of water.

Gwen glanced at the clock on the wall and realized she'd been talking for almost half an hour.

Evan handed her the bottle. "Sorry to interrupt. If you can come with me, we're ready to get started."

Gwen said goodbye to the people she'd been chatting with and followed Evan to an area behind the stage. Comfortable armchairs had been set out for Gwen and the other speakers. Governor Carlton sat in one of the chairs, deep in conversation on his phone.

"You can take a seat here. We're going to have have about fifteen minutes of presentations. We'll call you up first, then the Governor."

"Sounds good." Gwen said, taking the seat next to the governor. Despite what seemed like unbeatable odds, Carlton supported Gwen in being elected mayor, and the two became very comfortable allies. Gwen knew his presence at tonight's event was a result of their relationship. Otherwise, it was unlikely he would have made time to come out for a small event of this nature.

As soon as he hung up, Carlton turned to Gwen, smiling. "Hello, Madame Mayor."

"Governor," Gwen said, grinning. Beyond politics, Gwen genuinely liked Carlton and his wife, Constance, who had been instrumental in saving Val from a dangerous confrontation with former mayor, Roger Barton, endearing her forever in Gwen's heart.

"Listen, before they get started with us, I wanted to talk with you." The Governor shifted in his seat and lowered his voice, leaning closer to Gwen. "I'm putting together a task force for the Prevention of Violence Against Women and Children Act as part of that grant we just got. This is your platform issue, and I know you've been following our progress since we were awarded funds. I think you should head up the task force."

Gwen stopped breathing. Her head swam with possibilities. An appointment of this nature would be invaluable to her political career. Until a week ago, Gwen would have said yes without hesitation, but a tug in her belly gave her pause. Gwen had big plans for herself, and none of them involved being a mother, at least not yet. She'd hoped to run for governor before even considering a family. *I guess I'll have to consider it now.*

The Governor raised his eyebrows at Gwen, attempting to interpret her silence. "Gwen? Are you okay?"

"Yes, I'm sorry, Rex. I'm getting over a bug, and I'm still feeling a little out of sorts." Gwen took a sip of water, calming her nerves. "I must say, I'm a little surprised by your offer. Are you sure you don't want someone at the state level heading up the task force?"

The Governor grinned. "Positive. You're the right woman for the job, Gwen. Your tenacity in the election proved that."

The emcee for the event began talking into a microphone, creating enough noise that the pair paused their conversation. Gwen peeked around the corner and noticed the crowd had grown. She was impressed by the turnout.

Gwen turned back to face the Governor and, taking advantage of a break in the announcements, she said, "Can we get together next week to talk about the specifics? I'll be in Denver on Tuesday."

"Yes, absolutely. Can you come by around three o'clock?" he asked, checking his schedule on his phone.

"Of course," Gwen said, updating her own schedule. "I'll see you then."

As if on cue, the emcee began introducing Gwen. She reached into her bag and pulled out the folder containing her proclamation. She stood just as Evan appeared by her side to escort her onto the stage.

After reading the proclamation and making a few comments, Gwen was escorted back to the seating area while the Governor was taken on stage for his speech. Gwen sunk into the armchair, guzzling the rest of her water. Now that her part of the program was over, she could really consider the Governor's offer.

Since college, Gwen aspired to run for Governor of Colorado. And everything she'd done in her career so far had been to that end. Her years as councilwoman and now mayor, the volunteer positions she held, even her field of study in college had all been chosen with the specific goal of climbing the political ladder. Gwen wanted to change the world, and she truly believed in her ability to make a difference. The idea of leading up this task force was thrilling. But how could she even consider taking on something this big now?

Gwen rubbed her still flat stomach, trying to picture the little person growing there. What would becoming a mother mean for her career, for her goals? What would it mean for her relationship? Gwen had spent the last few months feeling envious of Val and John's impending marriage. Should she have the baby? And if she did, would she marry Jason? Would he even want to get married? Did she want to? Was it even necessary?

Gwen's breathing sped up, her calmness a thing of the past. Jason would be coming home tomorrow, and she had no idea what to do. Part of her wanted to tell him right away so he could help her figure everything out. Part of her was terrified of what his reaction would be. Would he leave? Would he stay?

Their relationship was already on the rocks, and this was a major wrench in the gears. Of course, there was also the part of her that wasn't completely convinced going through with the pregnancy was the best idea, in which case, should she even tell Jason? That thought made her feel incredibly selfish.

Exhaustion took over, and Gwen swooned a bit under the fluorescent lights and the stress of her situation. In an act of self-preservation, Gwen made excuses to an aide and headed out the side door to the parking lot in hopes of reaching her car before anyone stopped her to talk. She heard the crowd inside cheering enthusiastically, but all Gwen could think about was getting home.

CHAPTER TEN

Gwen woke up the next morning still feeling tired. She hadn't slept much, but luckily, ever since the hospital, the pain was gone. The doctor sent her home with instructions to eat a high protein diet, which would help with the nausea. Her follow-up with the OB/GYN introduced her to the exciting world of ginger chews and other natural ways to curb the queasiness. Easing the nausea helped a lot and, except for some vicious and random exhaustion, Gwen felt much better, at least physically.

Her emotional state was another story altogether. Gwen spent countless hours talking herself in circles.

I'm pregnant.

Oh, God, how can this be happening?

I can't be pregnant right now.

What about my job?

What if Jason and I break up?

I don't want to be a single mom.

But I've always dreamed of having children.

But I worked so hard to get elected. How can I throw that away?

Oh, my God, I'm pregnant!

Maybe it's a mistake?

She finally resorted to walking around her apartment saying, "I am pregnant" out loud, repeatedly, in a desperate attempt to reach some acceptance.

Gwen sat up in bed. *Maybe I'm thinking about this wrong.* For a moment, Gwen considered all the women in her life. Half her friends from high school and college had families, and many still managed to have careers. *Why couldn't I do this?* Gwen felt the sparks of her confidence trying to ignite. She felt almost optimistic when the phone rang. Seeing Jason's name on the caller ID, Gwen gave herself a second to take a breath before answering.

"Hey, honey," she said, stretching the stiffness out of her neck.

"Hi, babe," Jason said, and Gwen could tell he was smiling. "I'm getting ready to board the plane home, and I wanted to check in with you. Should be back in Cambria around two."

"Do you want to have dinner or do you want to rest?"

"Dinner!" he said, enthusiastically. "I can't wait to tell you all about this job."

Gwen smiled. It had been a while since Jason had been this happy. "Do you mind picking me up?"

"Not at all. I'll call you when I get home, and then we'll figure out where we want to go." He paused, and Gwen heard airport announcements in the background. "Okay, gotta go. We're boarding. Gwen …" he paused again, "I love you, babe."

"Love you, too," she said. She ended the call and put the phone back on her bedside table. She'd barely spoken to Jason since she'd been to the doctor. After telling him the doctor said she was fine, she avoided the topic, knowing the whole truth was not something she wanted to come out over the phone. For his part, Jason was so distracted with work he didn't seem to notice she was withholding information. Or, maybe she was in denial.

Fluffing up the pillows behind her, Gwen leaned back and settled into the book she'd been reading. She'd only made it a few pages when her eyes began drooping. The doctor advised Gwen to listen to her body, and she decided to start right away. Setting her alarm for noon, Gwen lay back down and was soon snoring lightly.

* * *

Jason got to his apartment a little later than he expected. Traffic through Denver was a nightmare, and he was tired when he finally threw his bags inside the front door. He made himself a cup of tea and stretched out on the couch, happy to be home, though the thought of seeing Gwen was met with trepidation. She'd been distracted the past few days, but he'd been so busy with training that their conversations were necessarily brief.

Digging his phone out of his jacket pocket, Jason texted Gwen to say he'd arrived home and was surprised by the immediate buzz that followed. He opened his messages and realized there was a new one from Alex.

Made it home. Yay! Can't wait to start work on Monday. Hope you made it home, too.

Jason smiled. He and Alex really hit it off. At first he'd been nervous he was playing with fire, but by the end of the week, they'd forged a solid friendship and working relationship. On Friday, they'd met up for dinner to celebrate finishing their training.

"We made it!" Alex had squealed. Her eyes twinkled, but Jason saw the fatigue in her face and shoulders.

"I'm going to sleep all weekend," Jason joked.

"I bet Gwen will be happy to see you."

Jason tensed. "You can never tell with Gwen these days."

"Uh oh. That doesn't sound good."

Jason shrugged. "Things have been rocky. I mean, we love each other, but I've been wondering if love is going to be enough." He sighed. "When Gwen and I got together, everything was high energy and positive. Gwen's that kind of person. But this job has really taken it out of her."

Alex nodded sympathetically. "I can imagine she has a lot on her plate."

"Yes, she does. But she's become almost impossible to be around. We barely see each other and, when we do, every little thing seems to start a fight."

Alex reached across the table and patted Jason's hand. The electric zing at the contact made Jason's heart rush a little bit, but it felt good to have someone care about him. "I know how you feel. Love was never a problem with my ex. I still love him. We just couldn't figure out how to make it work, and by the end, we could hardly stand being in the same room." Alex's expression was full of sadness.

Hoping to lighten the mood, Jason raised his glass of wine. "A toast. To new opportunities and new friends."

Alex's smile brightened her whole face. "To new friends."

Now, looking back on their conversation, Jason smiled. Alex was easy-going and understanding. She came from a pretty close-knit family in California but moving away left her feeling pretty isolated. Even after living in Salt Lake City for almost four years, she had no close friends. She seemed as relieved as Jason to find someone she could talk to.

Jason texted Alex back: *Just got here. Gonna sleep well tonight. Looking forward to working with you! Thanks for being such a great new friend.*

Sappy? Probably, Jason decided. But he was really grateful for the new perspective he'd gained on his training trip and a big part of that had been because of Alex. His phone buzzed again, this time it was Gwen. Instead of texting back, he called her.

"Just got home," he said when she answered. "I'm exhausted. I'm going to take a short nap and then I'll head over, okay? Should be around five."

"Sounds good. I've been lounging all day."

Jason felt a tug of concern in his stomach. Gwen wasn't the type to lie around, even on the weekend. "We don't have to go to dinner if you're not feeling well." Despite her reassurances that the doctor had found nothing wrong with her, Jason was still worried.

"No, I'm okay. Really. Just tired from a long week. I had that event last night and I decided today was a good day to rest. The doctor said I need to listen to my body." Jason heard the smile on her lips and he relaxed.

"I'll be there soon." They said their goodbyes and Jason set his alarm. An hour later, feeling a little more refreshed, he was in the car on his way over to see Gwen.

Gwen greeted Jason with more affection than she'd shown him lately.

"I missed you," she purred, nestling her head into his chest. Jason smelled the vanilla in her shampoo and every tender feeling for Gwen was rekindled. He wrapped his arms around her, hoping the moment would last.

"I missed you, too," he said softly, stroking her hair and keeping her close. When they finally let go, it was only to walk over to the couch and cuddle up again. Unwilling to move, it was nearly half an hour before they finally started talking about dinner.

"Do you want to grab something light?" Jason asked.

"No way. I'm starving," Gwen said, grinning at the look on Jason's face. "I know, it's been a while."

They drove across town to one of their favorite steak houses. The conversation was casual and easy. As they sat down, Gwen sipped on her Sprite, having declined a glass of wine, and asked, "How was training? Tell me all about it."

Jason launched into an enthusiastic discussion of the new company, with plenty of anecdotes about his co-workers, John and Alex, and his new boss, Bill.

"It's going to be such a great experience," Jason said, taking a bite of the salad that had been delivered to the table. "It looks like I'll be traveling almost every week, but should be home every weekend." Jason looked at Gwen to gauge her reaction. To his relief, Gwen was still relaxed, her expression content.

"That'll work. We hardly see each other during the week anyway." For some reason, this comment bothered Jason and he felt his shoulders tense.

Before he could stop himself, he said, "That's hardly my fault." Seeing the frown on Gwen's face, Jason kicked himself for getting defensive. The evening up this point had been so pleasant.

Instead of getting angry, however, Gwen seemed sad. "I know I've been difficult lately." She paused, and seemed to be searching for the right words. Jason's stomach clenched, preparing him for whatever bad news Gwen was about to impart. "There's a reason."

Before she said more, their dinners arrived. Jason and Gwen both plunged into their meals, relishing the reprieve from the direction the conversation had taken. Jason watched as Gwen polished off her steak with vigor. Despite the earlier tension, Jason couldn't help but say, "You weren't kidding about being hungry."

Gwen grinned, but the mouthful of steak she gnawed on kept her from speaking. They ate the rest of the meal in silence, though the tension dissipated. After dinner, as they headed back to Gwen's apartment, Jason said, "Gwen, I'm sorry, I didn't mean to pick a fight with you earlier."

Gwen sighed, but then she smiled. "It's okay. I know things have been rough lately. We should probably save any big discussions until we've both had a good night's sleep."

Jason agreed, though the mention of *big discussions* was ominous. When they reached Gwen's apartment, she hesitated at the door, as if she had something to say. But she remained quiet. Jason kissed Gwen, said a rushed goodnight, and headed home wondering whether they'd just shared their last moments as a couple.

CHAPTER ELEVEN

"You didn't tell him?" Val asked, unable to hide her disappointment.

Already feeling guilty, Gwen wasn't thrilled with this rebuke. "I know, Val. But things were getting tense, and I didn't want to tell him in the middle of a fight."

Gwen regretted her call to Val this morning. She'd hoped to gain some confidence for the day ahead, but instead she felt childish and selfish.

"I'm sorry. I don't mean to make you feel bad. I think you'll be able to work this out a lot easier if you bring Jason into the conversation. It's his life, too."

Gwen groaned. "Alright, Val. I get the point," she said more gruffly than she intended. "I'm going to tell him today."

Thankfully, Val backed off. "Good luck. Call me if you need me."

"Listen, please don't say anything to John for a few more days. I don't want Jason to hear it from anyone else."

"My lips are sealed," Val said as she hung up.

Gwen woke early, too nervous to sleep any longer. She noticed a funny pain in her hip when she lay in the same position too long. Having studied online articles about first trimester pregnancy symptoms, Gwen wasn't exactly surprised by the discomfort, though she wondered if she'd become a bit of a hypochondriac.

It was almost ten when Gwen decided she'd waited long enough to call Jason. He answered on the third ring, his voice sounding groggy.

"Morning, handsome," Gwen said, wondering if her tone was overly bright.

"Hey, babe. I just woke up. Ugh, is it almost ten?" Gwen heard the rustle of Jason's bedding as he got up. "How're you feeling this morning?"

"Pretty good." She paused to gather her thoughts. "Listen, can I come over in a little bit? I'll bring lunch." Gwen decided she'd better give Jason the news at home rather than in a public place.

Sounding a tad suspicious, Jason said, "Sure. I'm going to hop in the shower. See you in a bit."

* * *

Gwen arrived at Jason's apartment with sandwiches from the deli nearby, one of Jason's favorites. Seeing the logo on the bag, Jason frowned, feeling he was being buttered up for something he wouldn't like. After dinner last night, he'd spent a long time agonizing over his relationship with Gwen. First, he thought about how he would convince her not to leave. Then he'd wondered whether he ought to let her go. He'd gone to sleep feeling tense and hadn't woken up feeling any better.

Gwen went into Jason's kitchen and began pulling out plates and napkins. Jason brushed past her to pour some tea.

"Just water for me," Gwen said.

"Really?" Jason asked, more confused than ever. Gwen rarely drank water. She hated plain water. Iced tea had been her drink of choice since he met her. He only kept tea in his fridge for her.

"I'm cutting out caffeine."

"Doctor's orders?"

"Sort of. I'm supposed to cut down and that black tea has almost as much caffeine as coffee." Gwen distributed the sandwiches and opened a bag of potato chips. She seemed to be avoiding making eye contact with Jason.

"Gwen. Tell me what's going on," he finally said, exasperated by her constant motion and his own mounting tension. His words stopped her in her place.

Taking a big gulp of breath, she started. "Sit down." She took the seat across from Jason. "So, I left out a bit of what the doctor said."

In the pause that followed, Jason's mind leapt to the wrong conclusion. "Oh, God, Gwen. What's wrong?" He eyes began to prickle with tears.

"Oh, no, Jason. Jason, I'm fine. Actually, I'm pregnant."

Jason was completely silent, staring at Gwen with wide eyes. Eying him warily, Gwen stayed quiet and picked up her sandwich, taking minuscule bites. Jason realized she was waiting for him to speak, but his mind still reeled from the news.

After a few tense moments, Jason stammered, "Are you sure?"

Gwen laughed out loud. "Of course, I'm sure. My pain got bad enough Tuesday that I had to go to the hospital. They did a test."

"Wait, you were in the hospital?" Jason said, his face reddening. "Why didn't you tell me?"

"It wasn't a big deal. The doctor couldn't see me earlier, so they sent me to the ER."

Jason felt angry and shocked. Gwen's expression made it clear she was not happy with this line of questioning, fueling his frustration. "Of course it was a big deal, Gwen. We're supposed to be a couple, and you don't even tell me you went to the hospital?"

"Val was with me. If it had been a real emergency, I would have called you."

Jason drummed his fingers nervously on the table. "I can't believe this is happening."

Gwen frowned. "Are you really this upset about the hospital? You knew I was going to the doctor. Why is this such a big deal?"

There was a panicky edge in Jason's voice as he spoke. "Because you're keeping things from me, Gwen. Big things.

It's funny. I told Alex I thought something was going on, but she convinced me I was overreacting."

All the color left Gwen's face. "She? Alex is a woman?" She paused, as if giving herself a moment for this information to sink in. "This is the same Alex you had dinner with every night?"

Jason had the good grace to blush. "She's just a co-worker, Gwen. We really connected, and it was good to have someone to talk to." Jason looked down at his plate, suddenly the one not wanting to make eye contact.

Gwen's voice took on a dangerous quality, low, primal, something Jason rarely heard. "Why didn't you tell me you were spending all your time with another woman?"

Jason's eyes were pleading. "Gwen. Come on. It's not like that at all. Alex will be working in my division. We have a lot in common." With each word, Jason felt he was losing ground. *Shut up, shut up,* he scolded himself.

Gwen's expression was hard, cold. She'd stopped eating and sat rigidly, staring at Jason with a look that could kill. "Did you hear what I said, Jason? I'm pregnant. With *your* child, Jason. We're going to have a baby. And you spent the last week with another woman."

Gwen's words had the desired impact. Jason looked shattered. He just sat there, the words sinking in. So many thoughts were going through his mind. He wasn't at all prepared for the news Gwen delivered and he didn't trust himself to say another word. Things were bad enough already. Jason bowed his head, hoping to regain some sense of control over his world and was startled to hear the click of the door as Gwen left.

CHAPTER TWELVE

Jason must have looked like the walking dead when Val opened the door. The look of shock and concern on her face was plain. She ushered him inside and called John.

John Hatfield had been Jason's best friend since high school. He was one of the very few people Jason confided in. Since John and Val started dating, the two couples spent quite a lot of time together. Jason often felt pangs of jealousy when it came to John and Val. Their relationship seemed so effortless, though he remembered that wasn't always the case. Of course, Jason's feelings of jealousy were generally followed by guilt. He didn't begrudge John any of the happiness he'd found with Val. Jason wanted that kind of happiness in his relationship with Gwen, too.

"Are you alright?" John said, looking concerned. He handed Jason a glass of water and they sat down on the living room couch. Val disappeared into the back of the apartment and Jason wondered whether she was calling Gwen.

"No." Jason said, taking a drink of his water, unsure of what to say. "Gwen's pregnant."

For a moment, John's face reflected his shock at the news, but soon his expression transitioned into a wide smile. "Congratulations, man." He gave Jason a gentle punch on the arm, then chuckled. "Wow, I can't believe Val kept that one from me."

"It's a disaster," Jason said, his eyes beginning to glisten again. "She told me and then she flipped out."

"Why?"

"One of my new co-workers is a woman. We hit it off. I spent a lot of evenings with her." Jason looked at John pleadingly. "It was completely platonic. We're just friends."

John considered this new information. "And you brought her up with Gwen today?"

Jason bristled. "No, I talked about her a lot last night. But Gwen didn't realize that Alex is short for Alexandra." Jason looked down miserably.

John exhaled dramatically. "Did you explain that to Gwen?"

"Of course, I did. But then she left. And it didn't really hit me, what she said about the baby, until after she was gone. I thought she was going to break up with me. I didn't know she was pregnant." Jason paused, sipping his water. "I guess I made a huge mess of things."

After some thought, John said, "Well, I guess that explains why she's been so moody lately. And the stomach problems."

"She had to go to the hospital. She didn't even tell me."

"She didn't tell you she went to the hospital?" John said, his curiosity piqued.

"Not until today. Man, I don't know what to do." Jason leaned his head back on the couch and closed his eyes. "I'm going to be a father," he said, not looking up. As if his words opened a floodgate, tears began streaming down his cheeks.

John sat back, not sure what to do to comfort his friend. They sat like that for almost an hour. At one point, Val walked in and, seeing Jason's tears, shot a look of alarm at John. He mouthed the word *later* and she went back to whatever she'd been doing, giving the two men time and space to work things out.

Finally, Jason spoke again. "This is not the way I pictured it happening. I was going to marry Gwen, or at least I was going to ask her. I don't even know if she wants kids. She never talks about it. We've never talked about any of this. She must be a wreck. Oh, God, what if she doesn't want to have the baby?"

John smiled, reassuringly. "It's all going to be okay. You need to talk to her." John paused before adding, "But you might give her a little while to cool off."

Jason smiled weakly, wiping his face with his sleeve.

* * *

By the time Gwen got back to her apartment, she realized how badly she had behaved. She'd never been a jealous person, and Jason certainly never gave her any reason to doubt him, even during their roughest days. The mere mention of this other woman, Alex, had sent her into a rage. As soon as she'd left Jason's apartment, she remembered that he had, in fact, mentioned her quite a few times last night while talking about his new job.

As if things weren't bad enough, Gwen left Jason sitting there without a word. She'd gone home, put on her pajamas, and gone back to bed. It wasn't until she woke up that she realized what a coward she'd been through this whole ordeal. She'd been afraid to tell Jason about the emergency room visit because she didn't want him to come rushing home. Then, after finding out she was pregnant, she wanted some time alone to process. She'd sprung the news on Jason today and then run off like some scared puppy dog.

Feeling deflated, Gwen picked up the phone and called Val, the only person who could ever talk sense to Gwen.

"Hey."

"Hi."

"So, I take it things didn't go well?"

"Why do you say that?"

"Jason showed up on our doorstep a few hours ago, looking like he'd been run over by a steamroller. I thought for sure you'd call right away. Actually, I'm a little bit surprised it took you this long. What happened?"

"He didn't tell you?" Gwen wondered what Jason had said.

"I left the boys alone, but at one point, he was crying."

Guilt gripped Gwen's chest like a vise. "Oh." Gwen paused. "I told him."

"Yes, I gathered that," Val replied, her tone not exactly sympathetic.

Gwen sighed. "I told him, and then he got mad at me for not telling him about the hospital. And yes, I know you told me I should. And no, I don't want to hear any more about it." She breathed. "Then he brought up his co-worker Alex, who turns out to be a woman." Gwen couldn't keep the indignation out of her voice.

"So?"

Gwen bristled. She had hoped for a little more sympathy from her cousin.

"So, he spent every *night* with her!" Gwen's voice got louder.

"He spent the night with her?" Val asked.

"Not exactly. He had dinner with her." Even as Gwen said the words, she knew she was being ridiculous. "Every night, Val."

"She's his co-worker?"

"Yes. He says they're friends."

"For heaven's sake, Gwen. Since when did you become the jealous girlfriend?" Val's words stung. "What did he say about the baby?"

Gwen felt almost sick with guilt. "I didn't really give him a chance to answer. I left."

There was a long pause, and Gwen knew Val was counting to ten, her favorite tool for calming down.

"Wow, Gwen. I know this has been a shock. And I know how you feel about kids with your parents and all ..." Val paused. "Don't you think you're being a little harsh?"

"Of course, I am." Gwen's eyes stung with tears. "I was a raging bitch. God, this is so messed up." The tears began to flow freely. "I feel like I can't control my emotions at all. I fly off the handle. I cry all the time. How am I going to do this?"

Val's tone finally softened. "Gwen, you need to calm down. It hasn't even been a week since you found out you were pregnant and you're expecting to have all the answers. You don't have to, you know. You can figure this out as you go."

Gwen sighed. She knew Val was right, but she'd never felt so out of control of her life. "Is he still there?"

"No, he left about an hour ago. Said he needed to do some laundry before the week started. I guess he's flying out on Tuesday?"

Gwen realized she'd never even had a chance to ask Jason when he'd be leaving next. "I'll call him."

"Okay, good luck," Val said. The call ended and Gwen took a deep breath before dialing Jason's number.

He picked up on the first ring.

"Hey," he said, his tone guarded.

She worked up her courage. "I'm sorry, Jason. I'm really sorry for being so horrible this morning. I was so shocked by the whole thing, and I didn't want you to worry, so I waited until I could tell you in person. But my hormones are crazy and I get so emotional." The whole thing came out fast and furious, without a pause for breath. When she stopped, she waited for him to talk, her uneasiness growing with each second of silence.

"Can I come over?"

Gwen was taken off-guard. "I'm home."

CHAPTER THIRTEEN

Jason walked into Gwen's apartment full of apprehension. All the warmth he'd felt in seeing her yesterday had been obliterated by the stress of their earlier conversation. Gwen's eyes were red and puffy, and Jason saw tear tracks on her cheeks.

They spent a few awkward moments sitting on the couch before Jason started talking. "Look, Gwen. This isn't going to work if you don't trust me. And you can't keep things from me. We're either working together or not at all." She heard the pain in his voice. Jason wasn't the type to draw a line in the sand, but under the circumstances, she understood.

"I do trust you. I'm sorry I didn't tell you right away." Gwen was quiet for a moment, but it was clear from her expression there was more coming. "My feelings about being pregnant are all over the place."

"I know we've never talked about having kids, but I assumed we were both too wrapped up in our work to think about it," Jason interjected.

"It's not that." Gwen's face looked pained, and she seemed to be working up her courage for what was coming. Jason felt a ball of anxiety forming in the pit of his stomach. He tried to stay calm, but it felt like every conversation with Gwen lately had him preparing for the end of their relationship. He wondered once again if this was the moment.

"It's about me and my parents."

"Your parents?" Jason asked, confused.

"You know I'm not close with my parents. Part of the reason for that is they never wanted me."

"What? What are you talking about?"

"I was an accident. I overheard them talking about it once, and given their lack of interest in my life, it all made sense." Gwen looked utterly dejected and fidgeted restlessly. "I've never told anyone. Only Val knows because she was there. Anyway, even when I was small, I wondered why my parents didn't seem to care much about what I did. They gave me lots of freedom, but all I wanted was structure. Love. Thankfully, we lived near Val's family, and her mom was more of a parent to me than my parents ever were. I'm still closer to her than I am to my own mom and dad."

"I can't believe they didn't want you." Jason couldn't seem to reconcile this new information with the woman in front of him. Gwen was so full of life and energy. How could anyone not love her? He also realized that, from the moment Gwen mentioned being pregnant, despite all the drama, he'd already started thinking of himself as a father. How could anyone not feel that way?

"I'm really sorry that happened to you." Jason scooted close to Gwen, putting his arm around her and pulling her against him. She curled into his arms and he felt her sigh as she began to relax.

"I don't know why I never told you about it before. Honestly, I think it still hurts too much. I feel so ashamed, like there's something wrong with me. Like it's my fault that they didn't want me. And I've been feeling so stinking emotional lately. Sometimes I have to keep my mouth shut because my reactions seem so over the top."

Jason smiled. "I don't think you're alone. My mom says she cried all the time when she was pregnant with me." He felt Gwen chuckle, but when he looked down he saw the strain on her face.

"I'm not sure I'm cut out to be a mother."

Jason wasn't sure what to say. They settled into an uneasy silence. Before long, Gwen's breathing slowed, and he realized she'd fallen asleep, her head still resting on his chest. Jason let her sleep for almost an hour before helping her to bed and lying down beside her. Try as he might, sleep would not come. Gwen's last words still floated inside his head, fueling his anxiety. *What if she doesn't want to keep the baby?*

* * *

Jason packed the last of his clean clothes into his suitcase, barely conscious of his actions. His mind was on Gwen. They'd spent a few hours together on Monday and, though things felt relatively normal, they did not talk about the baby at all. Jason worried that if he brought it up, he might be faced with the bad news that Gwen didn't want to go through with the pregnancy. So, in what had become typical coping fashion, he avoided the topic.

Gwen seemed more relaxed, but distracted. They'd met up after she got home from work and had dinner. The conversation felt forced, with both Jason and Gwen making small talk but not delving into anything too serious. At the end of the night, Jason headed home feeling torn. Only the week before, he'd been so excited about his new job and the change in pace of his life. Now he wondered how his decision to take a high-travel job would impact the course of his life with Gwen.

A knock at the door brought Jason back to the present. Switching off the lights, he opened the door, handed his bag to the taxi driver and made his way to the airport. It was early, but the drive to the Denver International Airport was busy with commuter traffic. Jason used the time to check his emails. A message from his new boss waited with an urgent flag. On reading the message, Jason felt his stomach do a little flip. He was flying out to Western Division headquarters in San Francisco and, apparently, Mackey had assigned Alex to his project group, meaning they'd be working together every day.

His stomach tightened. Two days ago, he'd been willing to go to bat for his budding friendship with Alex. But something about working with her every day made him nervous. He had to admit she was attractive and very easy to be around.

You're being ridiculous, Jason scolded himself. *You're an adult. You're capable of controlling yourself. Alex could be a great new friend and right now, you need one.*

CHAPTER FOURTEEN

Gwen woke up Tuesday morning, raced to the bathroom and threw up. She sank down on the bathroom tile and waited for the nausea to pass, but after a few minutes she realized waiting was futile. *Ah, pregnancy.* She washed her face with cold water, relishing the shock of the water on her hot skin.

The pain Gwen experienced in the beginning had subsided pretty much the second the pregnancy was revealed. In its place was near constant nausea and unavoidable vomiting at random times. Her doctor suggested keeping ginger chews or crackers near her bed to nibble on before she got out of bed. Unfortunately, this was the second morning she'd woken up with no time to think before having to dash to the bathroom.

Padding back to her bed, Gwen picked up her phone from the bedside table. It was seven. *Jason should be in the air now.* For a moment, she considered texting him but decided to wait until later in the day. They'd left things unresolved but at least there had been no more fighting. Jason seemed so tense and Gwen was left to wonder how he felt, but was too scared to ask him.

Gwen had a plan for everything in her life, and having children was no exception. In her ideal world she'd get married, wait a few years, and then they'd discuss having kids. This had been her plan since her teenage years. She hadn't anticipated being single into her thirties. Focusing on her career kept thoughts of marriage and family at bay, until she met Jason.

Well, maybe before that. When Val and John started dating, Gwen felt an unusual craving for a love life of her own. She'd watched her cousin fall in love and felt pangs of jealousy. When Jason walked into her life, it seemed like everything was falling into place.

Gwen had to admit, as her relationship with Jason grew serious, she'd been more and more fearful of approaching the topic of marriage and children. Ironically that didn't stop her from feeling irritated Jason hadn't taken the first step. For the past year, she also spent more time thinking about her own parents and her childhood than she had in years.

Gwen's parents, Jack and Leann, had been married nearly a decade when they found out they were expecting. Leann had been in her mid-thirties and, as the story went, she cried for days when she heard the news. Gwen used to cringe when her mother told this story. Even as a little girl she understood something was wrong with the way her mother felt about her.

Gwen often wondered why her parents had gone ahead with the pregnancy, but they did. Gwen was born on a sunny spring day and her father walked out on her and her mother a few years later.

Leann moved herself and Gwen closer to Val's family. Gwen became a regular fixture in Val's household. Craving the love and attention she did not get at home, Gwen worked hard to please. She was a model student in school, acing all her academic classes and filling her after school hours with so many volunteer and extracurricular activities that, when she did have to be home, she easily spent most of her time in her room, doing homework.

Val's mother tried to talk some sense into Leann through the years, but despite her best efforts, Gwen's mother didn't take to motherhood. With growing resentment, Gwen vowed if she ever decided to have children, she would do better by them. Ever practical, she also acknowledged that planning to have children was the best way to avoid being overwhelmed.

An accidental pregnancy was not part of the plan. Gwen couldn't seem to get past that idea. Not only were she and Jason not married, but they weren't even getting along very well. How could they bring a child into such an uncertain relationship?

Luckily, Gwen had no city business to attend to today so she lay down, intending to rest. Unluckily, without another task to keep her occupied, her mind wandered back to Jason and the look on his face when she'd told him the news. Last night, she'd expected him to bring it up, but when he hadn't, she began to fear the worst. Did Jason even want to have kids? She couldn't remember ever having had a conversation with him about it. Would he leave her?

Gwen dozed fitfully until her alarm went off at eight o'clock. Still feeling nauseous, she opted for sweatpants and a day spent working at home.

* * *

Having had a fairly unproductive Tuesday, Gwen already felt out of sorts when she walked into City Hall late Wednesday morning. She made her way quickly to the council office, keeping her head down and praying to avoid another confrontation with Karen Fredrickson.

A few hours later, Gwen had just finished up a report when she heard a knock at the door.

"Come on in."

The door opened slowly and a beautiful bouquet of flowers materialized in the hands of Evan McDaniel. Unable to stop herself, Gwen blushed.

"Hello, Mayor Marsh," Evan's voice was shaky and Gwen saw color rising in his cheeks. He walked toward her hesitantly and handed her the bouquet. "The committee wanted to say thank you," he said, shifting his weight from foot to foot as he spoke, unable to make eye contact with Gwen. "For your help with our event," he added, unnecessarily.

Despite her own awkward feelings, Gwen felt a surge of compassion for Evan. *The poor kid is practically shrinking over there.*

"Thank you, Evan. I enjoyed it! You guys did a great job of getting people to attend."

Gwen walked to her desk, and placed the flowers gently beside her keyboard until she found some water. When she turned around, Evan stood nearer, closer than felt comfortable. His face was still red, but he wore a very determined expression.

"Ms. Marsh. Um…Mayor. Err, Gwen."

Gwen felt her jaw clench. She had a bad feeling she knew what was coming. "I wondered, if you wouldn't mind … I mean, I was hoping … you'd let me take you to lunch." Evan let out a big sigh, his posture deflating a bit with the escape of air.

Gwen had sensed that Evan had a crush on her, but she assumed once the event was over, there would be no reason for them to be around one another and therefore, he'd lose interest. Apparently not. She took a slow breath before speaking.

"Oh, Evan. I'm so flattered you asked me, and I really appreciate the offer, but I can't."

"Why?" The answer came so quickly that Gwen was caught off-guard. She hadn't pictured having to explain herself. The look on Evan's face was a mix of embarrassment and maybe frustration. Or even anger?

Gwen stumbled as she hunted for the right words. "Evan you're a great guy, but I think I'm much too old for you. And anyway, I have a boyfriend."

"That Jason guy?" Gwen was startled Evan knew Jason's name. His pouting tone only added to her growing sense of unease. She felt like she was reliving the very worst of her high school days.

"Yes, Jason." Gwen took a step back, hoping Evan would take the hint she was ready for the conversation to be over. Evan shoved his hands in his pockets and turned toward the door. Before leaving, he turned back toward Gwen.

"Thank you, Mayor Marsh." And before Gwen could

say another word, he left, closing the door a little harder than necessary.

CHAPTER FIFTEEN

The phone rang four times and Jason was getting ready to leave a message when Gwen answered. "Hello?"

"Hey, Gwen."

"Oh, hi." Her voice was groggy. "How was your day?"

"Good. Busy. I'm glad the week is over." Jason struggled for something to add, but came up short. He waited for Gwen to take her turn, hoping she'd have more to say but also antsy to get off the phone.

"Me too."

No such luck. There was a pregnant pause. "I wanted to check in before I head to dinner."

"Oh, okay. Have a safe trip home tomorrow."

"I will. Love you."

"Love you, too."

The week had come and gone in a blur of activity, but Jason had been reluctant to talk work with Gwen. Every conversation was superficial, giving him the impression of the two of them drifting further apart. He'd spent most of his weeknights moping around his hotel room. When Alex asked Jason to dinner with a group of other co-workers on Friday, he decided to say yes, looking forward to socializing.

They'd agreed to meet at the seafood restaurant down the street from Jason's hotel. Alex had family in the area, so she wasn't staying in the hotel this time. Walking into the restaurant, Jason was relieved to see Alex waiting for him wearing a frumpy sweatshirt and jeans, clearly a casual dinner date with a friend and nothing more. She looked tired, and he was glad he'd accepted the invitation. It would be a good chance to see how everyone's week had gone and to lend some support.

"Hey!" Jason said. Alex began to walk toward him and they met in front of the hostess podium. "Where is everyone else?" The lobby was now empty except for the two of them.

"Um, Phil couldn't make it. Something about flying home early for a doctor's appointment. John and Becca texted a few minutes ago saying they couldn't come after all. So. I guess it's just you and me." Alex smiled, her eyes seemed to glow with mirth.

Jason smiled back, trying to conceal his disappointment. As much as he got along with Alex, he'd been hoping to get to know his other co-workers, too.

The hostess led them to a table with a great view of the Golden Gate Bridge. Jason spent so much time in the office he hadn't noticed the San Francisco landmark was this close.

Alex leaned back in her chair and stretched. "I'm exhausted. I'm sure the pace will slow down eventually but this ramp-up is really wearing me out."

"I know how you feel. I crashed early every night this week."

"Did you get along with Steve in accounting? I only had to talk to him for about five minutes, but I didn't like him."

Jason smiled. "He can be hard to take. But we were working pretty well together by the end of the week. I think he's just a little socially awkward."

"That's good to know," Alex said, chuckling. "I'll reserve judgment until I've had a chance to get to know him better. Not that I'll have to work with him much. I think most of the financial data for the project will be coming from your team." The waiter stopped by to drop off their drinks. Jason had ordered a beer. Alex sipped a glass of red wine.

"So, you've got family here in town?" Jason asked, hoping to divert the conversation away from work for a little while.

Alex sighed. "Yes. My aunt and uncle live here. I've been staying in their basement, but I think I'm going to go the hotel route next time. They have three incredibly spoiled dogs who bark at all hours of the night."

"No wonder you're tired. I think sleep is going to be important in this job. With all the traveling and the changes in scenery, there'll be a lot of adjustment." Jason took a big gulp of his beer, frustrated he'd brought the topic back to work again so quickly. But then again, he was out with a co-worker so what did he expect?

"How about you? How's life at home? How's your girlfriend coping with all this travel?"

As much as Jason wanted to avoid talking about his job, he'd rather work another eight hour shift than talk about Gwen. Especially with Alex.

"Oh, she's handling it so far." Jason's mood darkened.

"Is everything okay?" Alex asked.

"Things are a little bit complicated at the moment." He paused, choosing his words carefully. "We're working through some tough issues. But I don't want to get into it right now. Anyway, we need to celebrate our first official week on the job." Jason raised his glass of beer to toast, forcing a smile to his face.

Thankfully, Alex veered onto safer subjects. They talked about common interests, hobbies, favorite restaurants. Before they knew it, they'd cleaned their plates and the sun had set.

"Wow, that really was the best seafood in town!" Jason exclaimed, rubbing his stomach for dramatic effect, which made Alex giggle.

"Have you had a lot of seafood this week?" she asked.

"No. Actually, this is the first time I've been out. I've been living on peanut butter sandwiches in my hotel room," he admitted.

Alex scrunched her nose disapprovingly. "You know, half the fun of a high-travel job is trying out all the local food at company expense."

Jason chuckled. "Good point. I'll have to do better next time."

"Great! Because we'll both be in Arizona next week. We can fill up on Mexican food. Yum." Alex's expression was one of total pleasure, which Jason found amusing.

"You're a fan, eh?"

"You have no idea."

"Then I guess it's a date," Jason said, though he regretted his choice of words the moment they escaped his lips. He glanced up at Alex, but she still gazed out the window at the boats in the bay, seemingly unaffected by his statement.

They split the check, said goodbye at the door and Jason walked back to his hotel, feeling conflicted again. He enjoyed spending time with Alex a lot, and something about that made him feel incredibly guilty.

What am I doing? He stepped up his pace, determined to catch Gwen on the phone before he went to bed and to get back on track. But when he rang her phone, it went straight to voice mail. He left a short message about his arrival time the following day, packed his bag, and went to bed.

* * *

Gwen popped another ginger chew in her mouth as she walked into City Hall for an early meeting. Though her nausea seemed to last all day, it was especially bad in the morning making these early meetings torturous. Not that they hadn't been before. Since taking office, the morning budget meetings had been fraught with tension. Karen's manner in dealing with the council, and especially with Gwen, had become openly hostile of late.

Gwen did her usual dash to the council office, hoping to avoid any contact with Karen before the meeting. The previous day's mail was laid out on the worktable in the middle of the room.

Gwen locked her purse up in her filing cabinet, made a cup of hot tea and sat down to sort the mail. There were a few letters from constituents, mostly addressed to her. She received twice as much mail as any previous mayor, which she attributed to having made herself so accessible to the public. The thought made her grin.

The grin was short lived, however. A quick glance at the wall clock reminded Gwen that it was time for the meeting. She gathered her notebook and headed down the hall to the conference room. When she arrived, Karen and her fellow councilman, Scott Harris, were sitting in the corner, talking in low tones with their heads together. Gwen's relationship with Scott was the shakiest of all her fellow councilmen. Scott had been tight with Roger Barton's camp during the election and a continued coolness permeated their interactions, though they'd so far been able to work around any hostile feelings. Scott talking so comfortably with the city manager didn't do anything to calm Gwen down.

You're being so paranoid, Gwen admonished herself as she took a seat at the other end of the table. As a council member, Gwen always felt confident in her role. As the mayor, the opposite was true. For the first time in her life, Gwen felt easily flustered and anxious about her role. Those feelings were amplified by her pregnancy. She imagined the headlines. *Mayor Gwen Marsh, Unwed and Pregnant.* It wasn't exactly the way she'd pictured herself.

Politics is perception, Gwen thought nervously. Would they ask me to resign?

A few minutes later, the other council members assembled. When the finance manager walked in, all conversation stopped and the meeting was underway. Within minutes, it was clear that, what could have been a very simple meeting, was going to be become a brawl. Gwen submitted her updated budget requests and Karen was determined to tear apart her proposals line by line.

"It's possible that our new mayor has forgotten restrictions on travel expenses were put in place after the election." Karen's condescending smirk sent Gwen's stomach tumbling.

"Not at all," Gwen retorted, trying to keep her voice calm. "I've reduced my travel expenses to only the most essential trips. I think you'll have to agree that particular line item is smaller than it has been in the past decade."

Karen shifted in her chair. "What's this conference in Denver on line thirty-six?"

"The annual Colorado Metro Mayor's Conference. Every mayor for the past twenty years has attended. Since its inception actually." Gwen's neck tensed. It was this back and forth that defined any meetings where both she and Karen were present. Gwen could see Karen gearing up for a response and decided to cut her off by adding, "I'm presenting this year on women in politics so my presence is not negotiable."

The smug smile plastered on Karen's face fell quickly. The lapse in the volleys gave the finance manager time to chime in.

"I don't think that's a problem. It's always good to have our city represented in state events," he said, effectively shutting down the subject. Gwen stifled a laugh, as she watched Karen's face droop like a child who'd been caught with her hand in the cookie jar.

After several more debates on expense items, all from Gwen's proposed budget, the meeting began to wrap up. *Not a minute too soon,* Gwen thought as she grabbed her notebook and sprinted to the restroom, leaving many bewildered faces in her wake.

She'd made it almost back to her office when she heard her name being called across the hall. Taking a moment to enhance her calm, Gwen turned to find Karen walking out of her own office and heading her direction.

"What can I do for you, Karen?" Gwen asked as sweetly as she could manage.

Karen frowned. "Are you feeling alright?" Gwen relaxed a little, about to respond when Karen added, "Not everyone can do this job. It looks like it's wearing you out."

Gwen sighed. "I'm fine, Karen. I'm sure you have work to do, so if you'll excuse me." Without waiting for a response, Gwen walked into the council office and shut the door behind her. She rested her back against the door and was congratulating herself on a narrow escape when there was a knock on the door. She opened the door to face the now glaring Karen.

"Look, Mayor Marsh. I understand this is a part-time job for you, but some of us have to work for a living. I'd appreciate it if you wouldn't blow me off."

"Oh, come on, Karen. Haven't we already had enough of this?" Gwen felt her shoulders slump despite her efforts to keep up a confident stance. "You've nitpicked my budget requests. What more can I do for you today?"

The sneer on Karen's face was reminiscent of the former mayor and Gwen couldn't help but cringe. "I simply wanted to inform you that next week's meeting has been moved to Wednesday at noon."

Gwen took out her phone and checked her calendar. "I can't make it, but I can have the modified budget proposal to Tom by Monday morning."

"I'm sure we'll get along without you." Karen turned and walked to her office, closing the door rather loudly behind her. Gwen retreated into the council office and sank into her desk chair. She was about to start packing up when something occurred to her. Picking up the phone, she dialed Tom in Finance.

"Lowry, Finance."

"Hey, Tom. It's Gwen. I wondered if you knew why the budget meeting next week was moved. I thought Scott and Jim couldn't do Wednesdays."

"It wasn't moved, Gwen." She heard him shuffling some papers. "Where did you hear that?"

Gwen's thoughts were racing. "Oh, I must have gotten my wires crossed. I'll see you then." She heard a click and realized that Tom hung up. Normally, Gwen would have been irritated by Tom's impersonal manner, but she was too busy thinking about Karen. Had there been a misunderstanding or was Karen now actively sabotaging Gwen?

CHAPTER SIXTEEN

Jason's flight got into Denver late in the afternoon. It was a short flight, but by the time he reached his apartment, he'd worked himself into a frenzy. Thoughts of Gwen, the baby they might have together, and the sudden shift in the direction of his life had him worked up. He and Gwen hadn't really talked about having children. It was obvious that Gwen's full focus was on her career and he wasn't in a rush to have kids. He knew Gwen was on birth control and so they'd gone about their lives without considering the possibilities.

Throwing his bag on his bed, Jason made his way into the kitchen and grabbed a beer from the fridge. He kicked back on the couch and tried to concentrate on the feeling of the cool, bubbly liquid as it slid down his throat. The relief was short-lived. His thoughts kept slipping back to Gwen, and he picked up the phone to call her, his fingers on autopilot.

"Hello?" Much to Jason's surprise, Gwen answered the phone, a rarity these days, but she sounded as if she'd been sleeping.

"Gwen? Are you okay?"

"What? Oh, sorry. I wasn't feeling well so I took a nap. I didn't realize it had gotten so late. Did you just get home?" Gwen's sleepy voice always made Jason smile.

"A few minutes ago. I know we weren't going to meet up 'til tomorrow. But I thought maybe we should talk."

Jason heard Gwen's sigh and he braced for a rejection. "We probably should talk." Unfortunately, this response was almost worse for Jason's already fragile nerves. His mind immediately started mapping out all the worst things Gwen might have to say.

"Want me to bring dinner?"

"Something light for me. I'm too nauseous for much. Maybe some soup."

Jason called in a to-go order, which included Gwen's favorite wonton soup.

On the way to Gwen's apartment, Jason tried to shift his thinking. His greatest fear was that Gwen would decide not to continue the pregnancy. Being a fairly progressive thinker, Jason supported a woman's right to choose whether to be pregnant or not. He acknowledged now that these previous feelings had been theoretical. Faced with the reality, he realized he really wanted this child. *Their* child.

But the decision wasn't his. He and Gwen weren't even married. What right did he have to tell her what to do? A tear slid down Jason's cheek as the gravity of the situation hit him. He should have asked Gwen to marry him months ago. He'd been nervous, afraid she wasn't ready, that she would say no. When Jason and Gwen started dating, she was an effervescent, relentlessly cheerful and determined career woman who'd landed the job she'd been dreaming of for years. Her enthusiasm and energy were infectious. But there was also something very guarded about her. Something he hadn't seen until months into their relationship. She rarely spoke about her family or personal life, and never voluntarily. When Jason suggested they fly out to Florida to meet his parents, she'd found excuse after excuse not to go.

In the meantime, his job at the city imploded and Gwen's job had become a daily struggle. Whether it was due to the stress of his work or Gwen's avoidance of his family, Jason decided this was a sign she didn't want that kind of commitment right now. A rationalization, he realized, that was intended to protect himself from heartache and rejection.

But now the playing field was completely different. Gwen was pregnant with his child and they were barely talking. The situation seemed hopeless. Jason could think of many reasons for Gwen to end the pregnancy, but he had a hard time imagining reasons she might decide to have the child. These thoughts were incredibly depressing and when Jason arrived at Gwen's apartment, he was almost resigned to the bad news he felt sure was coming.

* * *

Gwen slurped her wonton soup happily. It was the first thing in days she'd actually been able to eat with gusto and her feelings of goodwill toward Jason for providing her with one of her favorite dishes radiated warmth in her belly. Or maybe it was the soup.

"God, this is good," Gwen said, wiping a drop from her chin.

She glanced over to find a very mopey Jason picking at his salad without much interest. She could only imagine what he must be feeling, but then, she'd been so wrapped up in her own feelings she hadn't given Jason's well-being much thought. Her face flushed with shame. Gwen spent most of her time thinking about everyone else. How can I make the world a better place? How do my actions affect my constituents? Is Val going to get through this wedding without losing her mind? Yet she hadn't put much thought into her relationship with Jason, except when she felt irritated with him.

Why was that? She'd taken most of her frustrations over the past few months out on Jason, and he patiently stood by her. Well, not always patiently, but certainly steadfastly, never showing signs of wanting to break away from her. It was strange. Gwen had spent her whole life learning to take care of herself, to rely on her own skills and strengths to pull her through any obstacle. *That's not entirely true*, Gwen corrected herself again. Val was always right there with Gwen, willing to be pulled along into whatever mess Gwen thought up. She still felt a strong sense of pride and love for her cousin for helping her win the election.

"Gwen?" Jason's voice snapped her back into the present like a whip. She wondered how long she'd been lost in thought.

"Sorry. I've been thinking a lot about my life."

"Understandable," Jason said, though the expression on his face told a different story. "What are you thinking about?"

Gwen took a big breath, steeling herself for an emotional conversation that was way overdue. "I've been wondering whether I'm capable of having this baby, of being a good mother."

Jason furrowed his brow, a puzzled look in his eyes. "Why wouldn't you be?"

"I haven't exactly had great role models." Gwen leaned back into the couch, her hand resting on her stomach. "Like I told you, my parents didn't want me. Having me broke up their marriage. I barely know my dad and my mother only calls once or twice a year, usually when she's got some news to share. Or when she has an opinion about my life, like last year when she told me how ridiculous she thought my run for mayor was." She paused. "I always had Val's mom, but I guess I've been wondering whether bad mothering runs in the family."

"I know that can't have been easy on you. But you're not your mom, Gwen. What does that have to do with us?"

"I don't know. Nothing. Maybe everything. They got pregnant by accident. Neither one wanted a child but they went ahead and had me anyway. I spent most of my childhood at Val's house, wondering what I'd done wrong, why my parents didn't love me like hers did." A line of tears began sliding down Gwen's cheek, but she continued. "Have you ever wondered why you never see me talking to my parents. Or *about* them. Why I've been so reluctant to meet yours?"

"Actually, yes. I know you're not close to your parents, but

I figured you were busy or having conversations when I wasn't around. And I assumed you weren't ready to meet mine, to take that step in our relationship." Jason thought for a moment about his own parents. He didn't see them very often, but he knew they loved him. He tried to imagine what it must have been like to grow up feeling like your parents didn't want you, but the thought was too foreign.

"Now here we are, pregnant by accident. All I can think is, *when will he leave me?*" Gwen sniffled. "This isn't exactly how things were supposed to go. I don't know if I can do it."

Jason took Gwen's hand. "Listen, Gwen. We've been together for a year now and I feel pretty confident in believing that you can do anything." She smiled, which prompted him to continue. "I know I don't have much say in this situation, but …" The look on Gwen's face made him stop mid-sentence. She looked furious. He could see a vein pulsing in her strained forehead.

"What is wrong with you!" She nearly shouted, her face red with emotion. "What do you mean you don't have much say? Jason, this is *our* child. Of course you have a say in what happens. Are you serious?"

"Tell me how I was supposed to know that, Gwen. You've hardly been talking to me since you found out you were pregnant. You didn't even tell me when you found out. You waited days! What was I supposed to think?" Jason hadn't meant his words to be so harsh. Gwen's tears quickened, and he felt instantly guilty. He looked down at his lap and realized he still held Gwen's hand.

They sat in silence for a while. Gwen cried silent tears, still holding Jason's hand tightly. Jason breathed slowly, feeling the tension leave his body. *Our child*, he thought. *She said our child.* And for the first time since finding out Gwen was pregnant, Jason let himself hope.

Finally, after several more moments of silent reflection, Jason said, softly, "I love you, Gwen."

Gwen wiped away some of her tears and smiled, "I love you, too."

Maybe that was enough.

* * *

Things weren't exactly back to normal, but Jason felt like he and Gwen were finally headed in the right direction, together. They'd agreed to table their discussions about the baby for a few days so they could both get some rest. Having carried around so much stress for the past few weeks, Gwen was exhausted. But she seemed to be eating better, and for that Jason was thankful.

Jason spent Saturday doing laundry and relaxing. Gwen slept late in anticipation of an afternoon out with her friend Victoria. Victoria had been Gwen's campaign manager. Recently she'd taken a job in Denver and decided to move to the city to avoid the commute. Gwen still tried to get together with Victoria at least once a month, and Jason was sure she needed the girl time. They agreed to meet Val and John for dinner, so Jason decided to relax at home.

He was watching a movie when his phone rang.

"Hey, Jason." It was Alex. "I just got off the phone with Bill and they're changing the plan up for next week a bit. He's sending out an email but I thought I'd call to give you the head's up."

"What's going on?"

"The Arizona plant is a few days behind schedule, so they want us to fly in on Wednesday and stay through the weekend."

Jason sighed. "Okay. I'll call travel and get my tickets changed."

"Already did it." He heard the smile on Alex's face. "I'm going to email you the new flight and hotel info."

"Thanks for taking care of all that, Alex. I guess I'll see you Wednesday." Jason's tone was less than enthusiastic.

"You okay?" Alex asked.

"I'm resting. Still getting used to all this travel."

"I know. I had to drag myself out of bed this morning. But I hear it gets easier." Alex's positive attitude was one of the things he liked best about her. "Our flights get in about the same time on Wednesday. Want to share a cab to the hotel?"

Jason was annoyed to find himself blushing. It finally occurred to him that they'd be staying at the same hotel, probably every time they weren't in California. He reminded himself halfheartedly that Alex was just a co-worker. So, why was he blushing?

"That sounds good. I'll see you then."

Jason ended the call and sank back in the couch. He needed a reality check. He was clearly attracted to Alex on some level. That was normal, right? People were attracted to one another. It didn't have to mean anything. Besides, Alex had been very helpful and completely professional. They'd have to keep it that way.

Checking his email, Jason saw that Alex had forwarded his flight information along with hers so they could coordinate. Jason still felt pangs of guilt as he entered the information into his phone. He'd just returned to his movie when his phone rang again. He immediately started sweating before realizing it was John calling.

"Hey, man. Glad you're back in town. We still on for dinner tonight?"

"Gwen's still feeling pretty queasy so she wondered if we can go somewhere with soup. That seems to be her best meal these days."

John chuckled. "Of course. How about Joe's? They have good soup and salad. And steak!" John said, enthusiastically.

"Perfect." Jason said, his voice trailing off.

"Is everything okay?" John asked. Jason was sick of this question. He needed to do a better job of masking his emotions.

"I'm just tired. Gwen and I had a good talk last night but it was pretty exhausting."

"So you guys figured it out?"

"Sort of. We still have a lot to work out." Jason paused and decided to change gears. "Hey, John? Since you've been with

Val, have you ever been attracted to anyone else?" The moment he said it, he wished he hadn't. He heard the hesitation in John's voice, but John's response was kind.

"I'm not immune to other women," he said, but then added, "but no, not really. I've been too wrapped up in our relationship to notice much else."

Jason sighed. "Thanks, man. I needed to ask." He hoped John would forget he'd said anything. No such luck.

"What's going on, Jason?"

"Nothing really," Jason said without much conviction. "I think I'm stressed and not handling it well. My new co-worker Alex … I feel guilty whenever I talk to her. It's insane."

John waited a moment before responding. "With everything going on right now, it's not surprising that you're freaking out. But be careful."

"I know. It's really nothing. Look, please don't say anything to Val. I definitely don't need Gwen worried about this. It's a non-issue."

"No worries. We'll see you guys tonight."

Jason ended the call, feeling miserable. He should have kept his mouth shut. But, he needed to talk to someone and he was glad John was there for him.

CHAPTER SEVENTEEN

After an emotional night with Jason, Gwen looked forward to some fun with Victoria. She'd woken up queasy, but the more she was able to eat, the better she felt. It was pretty obvious that relationship stress had taken its toll on both of them.

Gwen arranged to meet Victoria at the mall midway between Denver and Cambria for some shopping and lunch. A little retail therapy always improved Gwen's mood. They picked up some Starbucks on the way in and Gwen tried not to notice Victoria's puzzled expression when she ordered a decaf mocha. As they walked past a dress store, Victoria squealed and dashed inside.

When Gwen caught up to her, Victoria held a sparkling peacock print cocktail dress. She thrust it in Gwen's direction.

"This is gorgeous! You'd look amazing in it."

Gwen looked skeptically at the very form fitting dress and crinkled her nose. "I don't know."

"What? It's perfect. You should try it on."

Gwen dodged. "You try it on, Vic. My stomach doesn't feel great. I don't want to squeeze into it and not get back out."

Victoria gave Gwen a long, contemplative look. "Hmm … did you see the doctor? Seems like you've been feeling bad for a while."

"Last week. Actually, I'm feeling a lot better today. Finally got some good food down last night. Jason brought over wonton soup."

Victoria smiled. "He's a keeper, that one." She put the peacock dress back on the rack, picked up her bags and they continued the walk down the mall.

Almost immediately, Gwen felt like someone was watching her. She peeked over her shoulder but didn't see anyone she knew. Still the feeling persisted.

When they reached the food court, they headed toward their favorite Chinese restaurant when Gwen did an abrupt about-face and almost ran into Evan McDaniel.

She put her hand on his shoulder to steady herself and noticed him flinch. "I'm so sorry, Evan. I nearly knocked you over."

Evan's face flushed, and he stepped back, shrugging Gwen's hand off his shoulder. "S'okay," he said and rushed away in the opposite direction.

Gwen stood for a moment, catching her breath.

"Who was that?" Victoria asked, stepping next to Gwen and watching as Evan fled.

"Evan McDaniel. You remember that voter registration event I did a few weeks ago. Evan's my university contact. He's a great kid." Gwen paused, remembering the deflated look on Evan's face when she'd rejected his lunch invitation. "You know, he asked me out after the event. I told him no. Haven't heard a word from him since."

"He certainly didn't seem very happy to see you."

"I know. But he walked so close to me. He had to have known it was me," Gwen said, sounding annoyed.

"You turned pretty quickly though. It took me a few steps to realize you'd stopped."

"Sorry. I caught a whiff of the food from El Toro and it smelled amazing." Gwen chuckled. "It's been ages since food smelled so good to me. Can we go there instead?"

Victoria nodded and they made their way to the other side of the food court for Mexican. Gwen ordered some enchiladas and was grateful to find that her stomach approved.

"That was so good," Gwen said, wiping her mouth and sitting back in her chair, placing her hand absentmindedly on her stomach.

"I guess so. You scarfed that down." Victoria's tone was amused but the look on her face made Gwen cringe. She wasn't going to be able to keep her pregnancy from Victoria long, especially given this erratic behavior.

"Okay. I'm going to tell you something but you have to absolutely promise not to talk to anyone about it." Gwen paused for dramatic effect. "I'm pregnant."

Victoria's expression remained calm. "Yep. I saw that coming."

"You what? How?"

"Come on, Gwen. I've known you for how many years? I've never once seen you order decaf coffee." Victoria started giggling and soon Gwen joined in.

After the laughter died down, Gwen said, "I haven't laughed like that in months. Jason and I have been struggling and then this happened. It's been a hellish couple of weeks."

"I can imagine. How did he take the news?"

"I did a pretty terrible job of telling him and then we got in a huge fight. We finally had a good talk last night but there's still so much to figure out. He took this job that has him traveling every week, so he's never around. It's complicated."

"Are you keeping it?" Victoria asked, very matter-of-factly.

Gwen sucked in a big breath, not prepared for this direct question. "Well," she hedged. "Yes. Though, honestly, I'm still not convinced I'm going to be any good at being a mother, but you should see the look on Jason's face when we even mention the baby. I never knew he wanted kids so badly."

"Maybe he just needed to find the right girl," Victoria said. But she still looked concerned. "You know, Gwen, this is going to change everything."

"I know. I really don't have it all worked out yet. I'm having so many problems at the city and I'm sure they're going to have a field day when they find out I'm pregnant. Karen already treats me like I'm useless. I'm worried they'll ask me to resign. And forget being governor."

"That's probably a little dramatic. There *are* female politicians all over the country who are also mothers. Are you guys getting married?" Again, the directness of the question took Gwen off-guard. She hesitated.

"I don't know. We haven't talked about it. It's funny. I've been feeling really jealous of Val and John. Val talks about her wedding plans and I want to scream. In fact, I've been a real bitch to Jason for the past few months. I kept thinking he'd propose and then every time he didn't, I lashed out. I wouldn't be surprised if marriage is off the table."

Victoria's face relaxed and she smiled at Gwen. "What about you Gwen? Do you want to marry Jason?"

"Yes, I think I do. But I don't want to get married because I'm pregnant. We have to figure out if we can even stay together given all the fighting lately. First things first. I need to figure out how and when to tell the world I'm expecting."

"No, no, my sweet friend. First things first. Breathe."

Victoria had always been good at keeping Gwen levelheaded. Gwen's enthusiasm and her take-no-prisoners attitude often caused her to leap before she looked. Victoria was a great counterbalance, and Gwen realized how much she missed working with her.

"How's Val taking the news? You've beaten her to the punch."

Gwen was about to answer when she glanced over Victoria's shoulder and caught Evan's face peering at her around the side of a nearby kiosk.

"That's weird. There he is again."

Victoria turned around as Evan's head bobbed out of sight.

"Hmm. Maybe he's more pleased to see you than I thought."

Gwen chuckled, but she felt uneasiness creeping through her system.

* * *

Jason picked Gwen up at her apartment and was surprised to find her looking rested. She wore a pair of faded blue jeans and a soft cashmere sweater, the one that picked up the green in her eyes. Jason loved that sweater.

"You look wonderful tonight," he said, giving her a quick kiss on the cheek.

"Thanks. I had a great day out with Victoria and managed to get a nap in after. I actually ate a whole meal today!"

Jason chuckled. "Are you ready for another one?"

"Actually, yes. I'm hungry again." In answer, Gwen's stomach gave a loud growl, making her blush.

"Let's get going then. We're meeting at Joe's."

"Perfect. I want a big steak right about now."

They made their way across town to the restaurant. Val and John were waiting in the lobby when they walked in. Val gave Gwen a curious look before wrapping her in a big hug.

"How're you feeling?" Val asked.

"Much better, actually. My appetite is back, and I feel like I haven't eaten in a year. I want one of everything."

John gave Gwen a kiss on the cheek and said, "We're at the right place then. We already put our name on the list so shouldn't have to wait long."

They chatted for a few minutes before following the host down to their table. Jason gave John and Val a rundown of his first full week at work, carefully skipping any mention of Alex. Every now and then he would glance at Gwen, who listened with rapt attention, a smile on her lips. Things almost felt normal.

"Sounds like the new job is a really good fit," Val commented. "Are you getting used to the traveling?"

"Not yet. I got some bread and a jar of peanut butter and ate sandwiches in my room most of the week. Starts feeling a little isolated after a few days, but I was too exhausted to go out."

"Are you getting along with your co-workers?"

Jason noticed Gwen's eyebrows rise slightly at Val's question. He took a sip of water to give himself time to plan his answer. "So far everyone has been really friendly. Of course, we haven't really gotten started with the tough parts. I'm sure there will be a few people who aren't happy to see me coming soon enough." He hoped that would satisfy Val's curiosity.

"Where do you go next?" Val took a sip from her glass of wine.

"Arizona on Wednesday."

"Wednesday?" Gwen chimed in, looking confused. "Short week?"

Jason grimaced, realizing her hadn't mentioned his change in schedule. "No. I have to stay through Sunday. The team is behind, but the reports have to be turned in this week so we'll be working through the weekend. Sorry, I just got the call today and forgot to tell you."

Gwen's disappointment was written all over her face. "That stinks."

Jason reached over for Gwen's hand. "It's a blip, Gwen. This shouldn't happen very often."

John shifted uncomfortably in his seat. A tense silence overtook the table, broken only when the waiter appeared with plates of food. They all tucked into their meals quietly. Jason watched Gwen cut up a few pieces of her steak, but after the first few bites, she mostly pushed her food around the plate.

Hoping to save their evening, Jason asked Val, "How're the wedding plans coming along?"

Val smiled at John. "Done. John's mom has taken care of almost everything. The wedding is less than two months away. I'm finally starting to relax."

John patted Val's hand. "She's trying anyway. You know Val. She's still worried about everything, especially all the guests. We sent out over two hundred invitations and are expecting maybe three hundred guests."

Val gulped audibly, causing Gwen to smile at her cousin.

"It's going to be so beautiful," Gwen said. "I'm pretty sure John's going to love your dress." Gwen winked at John. Then her expression turned sour. "Ugh, I hope I fit into *my* dress."

"You'll be gorgeous as always," Val said softly, though she wore a look of concern. "That reminds me. Anne has asked you and I to have brunch with her next Sunday. Will that work for you?"

"Of course," Gwen answered, though her expression betrayed a hint of anxiety.

"Don't worry. We'll do something simple."

"You haven't told her I'm pregnant, have you?"

"Of course not, Gwen. That's your news to tell in your own time."

Gwen sighed. "We'll have to figure out how to tell people, and soon. People are starting to suspect something's up. Victoria and I had lunch today and she guessed."

Jason raised an eyebrow. "Really?"

"Yes. I ordered decaf coffee." Gwen couldn't hide a smile at the memory. "I guess I'm a creature of habit." Looking down, she realized she'd placed her hand on her stomach again. "Oh, brother," she said, folding her hands in her lap.

Val chuckled. "Yes, those of us who spend a lot of time with you are bound to pick up on some things. Especially since you've been acting like you've got something to hide for weeks."

"God, this is all so overwhelming! I'm still trying to wrap my head around the idea that I'm going to have a baby."

Despite Gwen's obvious distress, Jason couldn't help but smile at Gwen's public admission of going through with the pregnancy.

"If I've learned anything about you, Gwen, it's that you're capable of anything." The smile John gave Gwen was so heartfelt, even Jason felt a rush of affection for his oldest friend.

Gwen smiled. "Thanks, John. I really appreciate that. This isn't the kind of challenge I'm used to facing."

"Listen, Gwen," Val interjected. "Let's get together tomorrow and we'll talk through this. Over pancakes?"

"Mmm. I miss pancakes," Gwen said, closing her eyes. "Ten o'clock?" Val nodded.

"If the girls are getting together, why don't we hang out?" John gave Jason a big smile.

"Perfect," said Jason, glad for the opportunity to have a long conversation about all the things going on in his life.

After dinner, the two couples said goodbye. Jason and Gwen went back to her apartment. Jason hoped to spend a little bit of time talking, but the busy day had clearly worn Gwen out. She was asleep as soon as she lay down, and Jason was left to his own thoughts.

CHAPTER EIGHTEEN

In the morning, Gwen was surprised to find a mug of hot tea and a plate of crackers waiting on her bedside table. A very energetic Jason sat at the foot of the bed, anxiously waiting for her to wake up.

Gwen smiled, sleepily. "Good morning, sunshine." She sat up and reached for the tea. She took a sip, inhaling the minty aroma, and sighed. "This is perfect. Thank you."

Jason grinned. "How're you feeling?"

"Not too bad." Gwen nibbled at one of the crackers. "I finally figured out that if I take my time getting up, my stomach doesn't stage a complete revolt. Of course, the crackers help." Gwen smiled at Jason while munching a few more crackers.

"I've been thinking," Jason said, hesitantly. "I think we should move in together."

Gwen paused, giving Jason enough time to start to panic. "Can we take a little more time to adjust to all this?"

"I need to be closer to you, to take care of you. And the baby." Jason tried to keep his tone level, though he felt heavy with disappointment at Gwen's hesitation.

"Look, I need some time to think things through. I don't want us to move in or change things in our relationship just because I'm pregnant."

"For God's sake, Gwen. Things *are* going to change." Jason couldn't hide his exasperation. "They already have. Our whole situation is different and avoiding talking about it or waiting to make a move isn't going to help."

Gwen took a deep breath before continuing. "I know things are going to change. I meant that I don't want to rush into anything without giving it some time. I'm finally starting to feel less stressed out. I need things to stay calm for a while so I can figure out what to do."

"What do you need to figure out?" Jason asked, fear creeping back into his voice.

"How to do this. How to be pregnant and be the mayor. How to have a baby and be the mayor. Things have been so stressful at work and I know this is going to complicate things. My whole career is about to go down the tubes!"

Jason felt like Gwen was pushing him out of the situation again. He felt anger rising and decided he'd better leave before things escalated.

"I'm going to go hang out with John. I'll call you later."

"Jason, don't leave mad."

"You know what, Gwen. You're not the only person this situation is difficult for. I don't want to fight with you, but we need to talk about this together. This is my baby, too."

Jason didn't wait for Gwen to respond. He walked out of the bedroom, grabbed his jacket and headed back to his apartment.

* * *

Gwen pouted between bites of pancake. "Why does he have to be such a big baby!" she said, searching Val's face intently, as if the answer was hidden somewhere in her expression.

"He's in shock too. He's taken this job where he's gone all the time, and no sooner does he start than he finds out you're pregnant. You didn't exactly break the news gently. He needs time." Val gave Gwen a sympathetic look. "And maybe a little more commitment from you."

"The thing is, we haven't been getting along well and then he took this job. I assumed this was the beginning of the end."

Val chose her words carefully. "Do you want to be with Jason?"

"I do," Gwen said, without hesitation. "Honestly, I think I've been self-sabotaging for months."

"Yes you have," Val said.

"What?" Gwen exclaimed, outraged.

"Come on, Gwen. Jason's been trying to get you guys to move in together for months. You've used every excuse imaginable to keep him at arm's length. I've never entirely understood it, to be honest. What're you waiting for?"

Gwen sighed. "I keep picturing my mom and dad. Do you think the inability to make a relationship work is genetic?"

Val chuckled. "No. I think your mom and dad failed you and each other, quite frankly. Maybe Aunt Leann never wanted to be a mother, but once she found out she was pregnant, she should have womaned up."

Gwen was shocked. She'd never heard Val talk so harshly about her parents.

Val continued, "Don't look so surprised." She reached across for Gwen's hand. "I love you, Gwen. My whole family loves you. We've never been happy about the way your parents have treated you. But we've also seen you tackle everything you've ever tried in life. Remember your fifth grade talent show costume?"

"Don't remind me."

"Your mother wasn't about to take the time out of her busy life to help you with your costume, and my mom was working on mine and Liz's so you decided to make your own."

"It was a disaster!" Gwen laughed. "My dress had a hole in the back. Everyone saw my underwear!"

"Yes, but you didn't let that stop you. You delivered your lines and took a big bow. You were so proud of yourself. I think this is the first time I've ever seen you so scared of anything."

Gwen took a sip of water and contemplated Val's words. "I've really never had to do anything that was this permanent."

"You're sure you want to go ahead with this pregnancy?" Val asked, very matter-of-fact.

"Honestly, I wasn't sure at first. Those first few days after getting the news, I seriously considered having an abortion and never telling Jason I was ever pregnant. It seemed easier than dealing with the reality. I went so far as to call the Planned Parenthood office and ask some questions." Gwen's face was pale. She never intended to tell anyone this story, not even Val. But talking about it made her feel more relaxed. "I talked to this nurse. She was so kind and caring. It occurred to me that my own mother never spoke to me with so much compassion. And I realized I didn't want my crummy childhood to keep me from having a family to love."

Val nodded, but remained silent, stroking Gwen's hand gently.

"Then, I freaked out. I asked myself if I was going forward with this pregnancy to show my parents that I was better than they were. Finally, Jason and I talked the other night, and I realized how much more he's invested in this relationship than I gave him credit for. I have no idea how things are going to go, but I do know that I want to have this baby."

"Then you need to let Jason in, Gwen. You can't keep throwing up this wall. It's not a surprise that he wants to live with you. If you're not ready for that, you need to be honest with him and explain why."

"I know. I'm such an emotional wreck right now. I get stressed out, and I can feel myself lash out, and it seems like I can't stop myself. I've taken to avoiding difficult topics."

Gwen closed her eyes savoring the safety she felt when she was with Val. "I think I pushed Jason too far this morning."

"Why do you say that?"

"You should have seen the look on his face when he left." Gwen sighed. "The first time he asked me to move in with him, he was clearly disappointed in my answer. But he seemed to get over it."

"Do you think he really did?"

Gwen pondered this question. "Maybe not. He kept bringing it up, and I always made some excuse. Same as today. I dodged instead of telling him how I felt." She paused. "It's not like it wouldn't be nice having him nearby. And I don't even want to think about having this baby without him."

Val looked at Gwen sympathetically. "I'm sure he'll come around. But you need to talk to him like you're talking to me now. Be honest. I think you can trust him to take care of your heart."

Gwen and Val finished their lunches, and Gwen headed back to her apartment to tackle the mounting pile of client work and city business that had amassed. *But first a nap.*

Gwen was becoming the queen of the power nap, having realized she could no longer muscle through the day the way she had before. Her attempts to do so resulted in missed deadlines and sloppy work; she was too tired to keep her mind on track. A few of her clients were starting to complain. The thought of losing business on top of everything else was not acceptable. No matter what happened, she still needed to be able to support herself.

*　　　*　　　*

Jason and John settled into a booth at a local sports bar and were making small talk over the game on the numerous screens scattered around the dining room.

"I heard their coach was fired for misconduct," John said, digging into the stack of nachos that had been delivered to their table.

Jason, lost in his thoughts, didn't respond.

"Hello? Earth to Jason? Are you with me?"

Jason shook himself back to reality. "Sorry, John. I'm having a hard time keeping my thoughts off of Gwen. We had another 'exchange' this morning. I feel like I'm on a roller coaster. When I think about being a dad, I feel like I could fly. Then something happens with Gwen and I feel like death." Jason picked up a chip, flicked off a jalapeño, and moved the chip to his plate.

"What happened this morning?" John asked, an expression of concern on his face.

"I asked her to move in with me. She wouldn't even discuss it." Jason's bottom lip stuck out in a classic pout, causing John to stifle a laugh.

"She's freaking out," John said. "Val brought me up to speed on Gwen's childhood. It's not surprising she's out of her element."

A guilty look swept across Jason's face, but the pout remained. "I know. We talked about that a few nights ago. I didn't realize she'd had such a crummy time. She never talks about her childhood at all."

"It's been interesting watching you and Gwen over the past few months. During the election, I truly thought her energy and optimism were impenetrable. She never got discouraged, even when Roger Barton was at his worst. But I'm beginning to see that her confidence at work doesn't entirely translate to her personal life."

"I think that's true. Anytime our relationship seems to be moving in the direction of commitment, she puts some distance between us." Jason took a big drink of his beer. "These past few weeks have been such a nightmare. When I applied for the job with BGB, I was one foot out the door with Gwen. I'd truly had enough of waiting around to see if she'd ever be willing to move forward with me. So what happens? She's pregnant. I feel like I'm being punished."

"Meaning what exactly? You don't want to have the baby?" John asked, raising an eyebrow.

"That's just it. The second I found out about the baby, I wanted it. I *want* to marry Gwen, and I *want* to have a baby with her. More than I ever wanted anything. And I thought maybe Gwen would want that too, but then this morning it seemed like she's still on the fence about whether she even wants the baby." Jason was in full rant mode, but he realized this last statement was more a projection of his own fears than a realistic interpretation of what Gwen had said. He scolded himself for being so dramatic.

They sat in silence for a few minutes. Jason's eyes move toward the screen, seeking some distraction from his tormented thoughts. But before long, John spoke again. "Give it time, Jason." Then John frowned. "So what's up with the questions about being attracted to other women?"

Jason sighed. He'd known John wouldn't let that question go, and once again, he kicked himself for having brought it up.

"You remember me talking about my co-worker, Alex?" John nodded. "During training we spent a lot of time together. She's a really great person, and I enjoy being around her. But we're just friends." Jason paused, planning his explanation carefully. "At least, I think we are. Ever since Gwen went off on me about Alex, I've been feeling really weird about her. I pretty much avoided her all last week. And, when we did hang out the last night in California, I felt guilty every time I found myself enjoying the evening."

"Why?"

"That's the million-dollar question. Alex is attractive and smart, but I hadn't considered her as anything more than a friend until Gwen freaked out. Now, I feel like I'm doing something wrong every time I look at her."

"Guilty conscience?" John asked, smiling.

Jason smiled too. "Maybe. It's so easy being around Alex. And now I keep noticing how cute she is. I don't mean to, and it's driving me crazy."

"You're flipping out because life at home is hard right now." Then John added, thoughtfully, "Is she interested in you?"

"I don't think so. I think she's interested in being friends. It sounds like she's been pretty lonely in her life. I can relate."

John's expression was sympathetic, but he still said, "Just be careful. The stakes are pretty high right now."

Jason sighed. "That's exactly my problem. I feel like I'm walking on the edge of a cliff and one tiny misstep will send me over the edge."

"Whoa. You don't think that's a little bit overly dramatic?" John said, laughing.

Jason couldn't help but laugh too. "I feel like a flipping teenager right now. My emotions are all over the place. I could live without all the high school drama."

"Understandable. But I think the situation with Gwen is pretty serious. You need to keep your eye on the important stuff."

Jason nodded. He sat back with his beer in hand and turned his attention to the game. John was blunt, and his words hit a nerve with Jason. But he was right. Jason had allowed himself to be distracted by Alex when he needed to try hard on working things out with Gwen.

When the game ended, John and Jason parted company. Jason headed back to his apartment, wondering how Gwen's morning with Val had gone. He knew they'd need to talk seriously about the baby and their relationship, but he resolved to try not to push Gwen too far too fast. Maybe she was right, they needed to proceed cautiously. Avoid rash decisions. He spent the afternoon attempting to remain calm.

CHAPTER NINETEEN

Jason and Gwen continued to avoid any serious discussion about their relationship, or at least Gwen hadn't brought it up, and Jason had been too afraid to rock the boat to initiate any further conversation. Gwen went back to work, and Jason spent his days preparing for the weekend audit. On Tuesday night, Jason cooked dinner for Gwen at his apartment. They'd decided to spend a relaxing evening at home since Jason would be out of town for the rest of the week.

"This is delicious," Gwen said, closing her eyes as she enjoyed her last bite of pasta. "I should make you cook every night." Gwen grinned at Jason, who scooped up the last of the sauce on his place with a piece of garlic bread.

"I'd like that." Jason watched Gwen's expression, wondering if this hint of his domestic intentions would sour her mood, but she seemed to take his comment in stride.

"I wonder how this brunch with Anne and Val on Sunday is going to go. I've been a miserable maid-of-honor. It's been so hard lately. But I need to plan Val's shower. The wedding is six weeks away." Gwen's tone was relaxed, but Jason could see worry lines appear around her eyes.

Moving around to stand behind her, Jason put his hands on her shoulders and massaged gently. He could feel her muscles relax. "It's all going to work out, Gwen. You know Val, she probably doesn't even want a shower."

Gwen chuckled. "She's so stressed about the wedding that it hasn't even come up in the conversation. But Anne wants to have a party for all the society ladies so I need to get back on the ball. Val may not want a shower, but she definitely wants to make Anne happy."

Still rubbing her shoulders, Jason said, "I'm planning a stag night for John the night before the wedding. I never thought John would go for it, but his whole demeanor seems to have changed since meeting Val."

Gwen turned to face Jason. "I know what you mean. He went from reclusive to man about town overnight. At least, he doesn't seem to mind being out in public as much. He even appeared at a ribbon cutting the other day with Roger Barton. You know that couldn't have been pleasant."

Since the election, the former mayor disappeared from public politics. But his fingers could still be felt in city government, especially in terms of the resistance Gwen faced from some of his cronies. Karen Fredrickson was the worst. Karen had never been a fan of Barton's, but for some reason, her animosity toward Gwen and Jason had grown like a weed since he'd left office.

"Did I tell you Karen is actually trying to sabotage me now? And she's not being subtle."

Jason sat down again. "No. But I can't say it's surprising. She was openly hostile to me before I left, even in front of Tom. What did she do?"

"She told me the budget meeting had been rescheduled next week so I would miss it. Luckily, I called Tom right away because the change didn't make any sense. Bet she'll be surprised when I show up at the meeting. She attacked every budget item I submitted at the last meeting. Who knows what she would've tried to get away with without me there."

Jason sighed. "I don't even remotely miss working there, but I do wish I were around more to support you."

Gwen reached for his hand. "Thanks, babe. I need to figure out what's driving Karen's animosity. I've only been in office a year, and I'm already wondering if I will make it through my term. Something's gotta give. And when she finds out I'm pregnant, Karen's going to use it as ammunition. I need to figure out a few things before we go public."

It was the first time the conversation touched on the pregnancy, and Jason fought the urge to take it further. Instead he squeezed Gwen's hand and said, "I'm sure you'll work it out. I'll help any way I can."

Gwen left early, giving Jason time to pack and get to bed. His flight to Arizona was scheduled for 6:00 AM. He set his alarm and went right to sleep for the first time in weeks.

The next morning, Jason arrived in Arizona and was surprised to find Alex waiting for him at the gate. He'd spent the flight trying to figure out how to manage their friendship in a way that didn't leave him feeling guilty all the time, but decided the best thing to do was to keep things casual. They walked to baggage claim, retrieved their suitcases, and got a taxi to the hotel.

After unpacking, they met in the hotel restaurant for lunch.

"We're not due in the office until two o'clock. I was thinking about checking out the art district. There are supposed to be some great galleries. Want to come with me?"

Jason hesitated as his internal struggle raged. Sightseeing with a friend was definitely not something he should feel guilty about. Yet, how would Gwen react if she knew he was already going out with Alex?

Hedging, he said, "I should probably review the reports before this afternoon."

Alex bumped his arm with hers. "Come on. We're going to be here until Sunday. Might as well check out the town. And wait 'til you hear what I have lined up for Saturday night!"

Jason's curiosity was piqued despite the slight irritation he felt about Alex's presumptive scheduling of his time. "What's going on Saturday?"

"The Arizona Taco Festival!" Alex squealed with excitement, and Jason couldn't help but laugh.

"Taco festival?"

"I told you. I'm a Mexican food addict. You said you'd join me. Imagine my surprise when I found out the festival was happening this weekend!"

Jason relented. "Sounds tasty. You know what, those reports can wait. I need to start relaxing or this job is going to kill me. Let's go see some southwestern art."

Alex looped her arm through Jason's as they walked out of the lobby.

* * *

By Saturday evening, Jason looked forward to being out of the office, even if he still felt a little awkward about spending time with Alex. During the week, they'd had several lunches together, but the audit kept him busy, and he was able to easily duck out of dinner invitations thanks to late nights in the office.

As the elevator doors opened, Jason saw Alex waiting across the lobby, her back to him. She wore a red dress that left little to the imagination. Jason felt his body react and was tempted to turn around and head right back to his hotel room, making whatever feeble excuse came to mind, when Alex turned around and spotted him. Jason put his hands in his jeans pockets and walked toward her.

"I already called a cab," she said, wrapping her arm through him elbow and leading him toward the entrance.

Jason's discomfort grew at the closeness, but he didn't want to offend her by pulling his arm away. Instead, he walked stiffly beside her. Thankfully, the taxi pulled up as soon as they exited the hotel. Jason was able to break away on the pretense of opening the door for her.

As the cab pulled away from the curb, Jason looked out the

window at the passing buildings, trying hard to lose himself in the southwestern architecture and the desert landscape.

"How's the audit coming?" Alex's voice was unnerving.

Turning to look at her, Jason said, "It's done. I have to finish up some formatting tomorrow morning, then it's ready for Bill." He was careful to keep his hands folded in his lap, ashamed at the traitorous way his body responded to Alex.

Alex smiled, seemingly oblivious to his discomfort. "I ate a tiny lunch. Saving up all my stomach space for tacos!"

It was difficult not to get caught up in her enthusiasm, and Jason wondered, not for the first time, if he'd ever be able to relax in this friendship. "I'm excited to see what a taco festival looks like. I've been to some great beer festivals in my day, so I'm expecting big things here."

"They have something like forty vendors selling various types of tacos and other Mexican food. It's a dream come true!"

Jason saw the cab driver smile as he looked back at Alex in the rear view mirror.

When they arrived at the festival, Jason was astounded to see a huge crowd. Every food truck or vendor stall had an incredibly long line. He followed Alex as she bounded toward a street taco vendor that seemed to have the longest line.

"Might as well start with the most popular, eh?" she asked.

Jason noticed several men taking Alex in. The breeze blew her dress in waves, drawing attention to her long tanned legs. She'd chosen a pair of strappy sandals that were very sexy.

Stop looking, Jason prodded himself as they moved through the line. After the first booth, they found a bench, polished off their first round of tacos, and went in search of the next taco fix. It didn't take long for Jason to get into the spirit of things. The food was exquisite.

The sun began to set over the Arizona mountains, creating rich bands of color across the horizon. Jason and Alex made their way to the festival plaza where a band was setting up.

They found a few free seats, and Alex sent Jason off in search of drinks.

He returned with two glasses of lemonade. Handing one to Alex, Jason said, "This is great. I'm so glad we came!" His earlier discomfort faded, leaving him feeling relaxed and happy.

"Me too," Alex said between sips of lemonade. Despite the heat of the day, the air became crisp as the sun went down. Jason saw goose bumps on her upper arms.

"Cold?"

"A little. I have a sweater in my bag, but I'm not ready for it yet. The breeze helps takes the edge off of my post-gorge sleepiness." Alex laughed.

"I know what you mean. I think I've eaten more tonight than I did all week. It was all amazing. I didn't know tacos came in so many varieties."

"You have much to learn, young man," Alex teased.

The band began to play and before they knew it, the plaza was full of people dancing. Jason was amazed to see old couples cutting a rug like they were teenagers, gazing into each other's eyes passionately. He hoped he and Gwen would be that happy as they got older.

"May I have this dance?" He turned to see an older gentlemen stretching his hand out to Alex. "As long as your husband doesn't mind."

Alex saved him from stammering a response by saying, "Oh, we're just friends. I'd love to." She got up and was soon being swirled around the dance floor. Jason couldn't help but feel a twinge of jealousy as he watched Alex's partner spin her effortlessly. After the first song, a slower ballad began. Jason watched as Alex's dance partner wrapped his arms around her, holding her close. Alex smiled, and the two talked through the dance.

When Alex returned to her seat, her skin was flushed.

"That man certainly can dance," she said, breathlessly.

"You two looked amazing," Jason said, smiling. "You should have seen all the other men watching you."

Alex smiled at Jason coyly, and Jason felt another rush of blood to his cheeks. He felt out of place. *What am I doing here?*

Attempting to regain some control over his emotions, Jason said, "I'm getting tired. Are you ready to head back?"

Alex's smile faltered, but she recovered quickly. "Sure. But don't you want to dance one song first? It's a lot of fun."

"I'm not much of a dancer," Jason said, feeling foolish. Alex's question was innocent, but his thoughts were not, and, sensing the danger he was in, he didn't trust himself to be close with her.

Seeming to sense his discomfort, Alex smiled. "I'm tired too. Let's go figure out where we can catch a cab back." She stood and waited for Jason to join her before heading back toward the street where they'd entered the festival. Luckily, a row of cabs waited nearby.

They made the trip back to the hotel in silence. In the elevator, Jason smiled and said, "Thanks for hanging out tonight. The festival was fun."

Alex grinned. "Thanks for coming with me. It's nice to have someone to do these things with." The elevator dinged as they reached her floor. She moved toward the door, but turned at the last minute. Rising up on her toes, she kissed Jason lightly on the cheek. "Good night."

CHAPTER TWENTY

The week flew by without any major hiccups. By Sunday morning, Gwen was happily anticipating Jason's return to Cambria. But first, she had brunch with Val and Anne Hatfield. With Val's wedding approaching, Gwen had a feeling she'd be leaving brunch with a long list of to-do's. But for the first time in weeks, she felt equal to the task.

Val picked Gwen up at 9:30, and they drove across town to meet Anne. They were surprised to find John's sister June sitting beside Anne in the restaurant lobby.

"June!" Val walked up to her soon-to-be sister-in-law and gave her a big hug. June had scrutinized Val with an eagle-eye when they first met, making Val incredibly nervous. But, luckily, they'd warmed up to each other quickly. June was an attorney and recently moved from New York to Seattle to become a managing partner at her firm's new west coast office.

"Hi, Val," June said, smiling. "Hey, Gwen. It's so great to see you." June offered Gwen a hug, and Gwen marveled at how easily John's family accepted her into their ranks. She thought about John's good fortune at having been born into a family that was so warm and supportive, with a little twinge of envy.

Anne stepped away from Val's embrace and took Gwen by the shoulders. "Gwen, I'm so proud of all the work you're doing. I've been hearing so many good things about you. Seems like you've really taken to the role of mayor."

Gwen smiled. "Thank you, Anne. It doesn't feel that way sometimes."

"John told me about the problems you've been having with the staff. It's a shame the path for women in politics seems to be littered with such obstacles."

Anne's words bolstered Gwen's confidence. She'd always admired Anne Hatfield, whose work in the community was nothing short of prolific. "I really appreciate your vote of confidence, Anne. The last few months have been really stressful. But I'm hoping to get to the bottom of some of the resistance I've been met with. And I'm presenting on women in politics at the Mayor's Conference so I get to address some of those issues."

The women made their way to a table on the restaurant patio. It was fall, but the weather had been unusually warm making outdoor dining a real pleasure. The sun shone brightly through the changing leaves of the trees, causing shadowy patterns to dance across the table. A slight breeze kept the customers from overheating in the warm rays.

When the waiter came, Anne ordered a round of mimosas.

"Water for me. And a cup of hot tea would be nice. Mint if you have it," Gwen said. When she turned her attention back to the table, she noticed Anne watching her. She stifled a groan when she realized her hand had migrated to her stomach again. She reached for her water as casually as possible, taking a sip and pretending to be fascinated with the leaves of a nearby tree.

"Are you feeling well, Gwen?" Anne asked. "Val said you've been having some health issues."

With a glance at Val, Gwen said, "I'm fine. My stomach's been giving me trouble the past few weeks so I'm treating it with kid gloves."

"I know how you feel," June interjected, much to Gwen's relief. "The stress of opening this new office is unlike anything I've ever experienced before. The opportunity was something I couldn't pass up, but between all the administrative work and knowing absolutely no one, it's been horribly lonely. I don't even have a secretary yet. I've finally started playing old episodes of Matlock in the background on my computer to have people talking around me." June laughed, but she looked tired. "I'm surrounded by tons of great restaurants and coffee houses, but I never seem to have much of an appetite."

Anne put her hand on June's arm, then turned toward Val. "Actually, Val. June has decided to come down to Cambria for a few weeks right around the wedding. I wanted to see if we could postpone the shower until she gets to town."

Val nodded, then turned to Gwen. "That'll work, right?"

"Of course."

"I'm looking forward to helping with the last minute touches on the wedding," June said. "My mother is starting to wonder whether this is the only wedding she'll ever get to plan." June gave her mother a playful look.

Anne smiled. "You and David certainly are taking your time. Though I never thought John would be my first child to get married." Anne winked at Val conspiratorially.

Val laughed. "Believe me, Anne. Until the election, I never would have imagined even seeing John out in public, much less marrying him."

"I'm happy he met you, Val," June said, beaming at Val. "I've always wanted a sister."

Gwen felt a stab of jealousy and inadvertently plunked her fork down loudly on her plate. Val looked at Gwen in concern. "Are you okay?" Gwen was relieved that Val seemed oblivious to Gwen's true feelings. She would have been so ashamed for Val to know how much she envied Val's situation.

"Sorry. I've been immensely clumsy lately." Another raised eyebrow from Anne convinced Gwen there was no point carrying on the charade. Anne was incredibly perceptive, and Gwen decided this would be a good place to test out her news.

"Not to take away from wedding talk, but I have some news.

Since I seem to be incapable of acting like my normal self, I'd better share it and get it over with." Gwen saw Val's look of surprise, and, for a split second, she wondered if this was a good idea. But she decided to plow forward. "I'm pregnant. I just found out a couple of weeks ago. It wasn't planned, and I'm absolutely terrified about what's going to happen as people start finding out. But there you have it." Gwen sank back in her chair, scanning the other faces at the table for a reaction. Val took her hand and gave it a squeeze.

Anne was the first to break the silence. She smiled. "Congratulations, Gwen. Is Jason excited?" Anne had been like a second mother to Jason, who'd grown up with John.

"He is, though I haven't made it easy on him. It's been such a shock, and then, with all the stress at work, I've been pretty cranky." Gwen looked down at her plate. "I'm so scared."

"Scared?" Anne asked, though her expression conveyed understanding, which made Gwen feel calmer.

"I didn't have the greatest childhood. I'm not sure if I'll be a good mother. Plus, I'm the first woman to be elected mayor of Cambria, and I feel like I've had to overcome so many stereotypes. Being unwed and pregnant wasn't how I'd imagined myself."

Anne chuckled. "That's a pretty dismal view. Though I do understand why you're feeling overwhelmed. People will have opinions, and they won't always be nice." She glanced at Val. "We've all gotten a good dose of how nasty politics here in town can be."

June chimed in. "To hell with people!" Her exclamation received a stern look from her mother. "I'm sorry, Mother, but this is exactly what's wrong with the world. Gwen should be celebrating. Instead, she's worried about what people will think about a decision that has nothing to do with them."

Anne sighed. "You know it's not that simple, June. But I don't disagree." Taking Gwen's hand, she continued. "I know this isn't what you planned Gwen, but children are a blessing. And no one who's seen you in action would ever doubt your ability to do anything you put your mind to. You'll always have my support."

Once again, Gwen was taken aback by the kindness and compassion she'd been given. She wondered how her own mother would react to the news. It had been months since they'd spoken, and their conversations were never very substantial. Unbidden, she felt tears welling up in her eyes.

"You have no idea how much that means to me." Gwen was horrified to feel a rogue tear escape down her cheek. Dabbing at her eyes with her napkin, she said, "I'm so sorry. I can't seem to keep my emotions in check these days."

Anne grinned. "The joy of motherhood. I cried all the time!"

June raised a glass. "To Gwen's baby and all the wonderful possibilities the future holds."

Val and Anne joined in the toast, and soon all four women were engaged in an animated conversation that left Gwen feeling a strong sense of belonging.

When she and Val got back to the car after brunch, Val turned to Gwen and smiled. "That was incredibly brave, Gwennie."

"I'm sorry if I stole your spotlight, Val. The morning was supposed to be about you."

"Not to worry. I'm sure there'll be enough 'me' stuff in the next few months to send me running for the hills." Val laughed, and Gwen was relieved to see that Val wasn't mad. "So, Jason's home tonight?" Her words were met with silence.

Gwen peered out the window at the front of the restaurant. "Gwen?"

Squinting against the sun streaming through the windshield, Gwen kept staring at the restaurant, though she wasn't quite sure about what she'd seen. As Anne and June made their way across the parking lot, she swore she saw Evan McDaniel peek around the corner of the building, following them with his gaze. Gwen shivered.

"Gwen? What's wrong?" Val's voice was full of alarm.

Turning her attention back to Val, Gwen said, "I don't know. Do you remember Evan? The one I did the voter event with?"

"Yes, the college kid. The awkward one."

"Mm hmm. He showed up twice during my day with Victoria last weekend, and there he is again by the restaurant." Gwen pointed toward the retreating figure. "He was watching Anne and June. It gives me the creeps."

Having had a run-in with the former mayor during Gwen's campaign, Val was still jumpy. "You think he's following you?"

Still distracted, Gwen said, "I don't know. It might be a coincidence."

They drove back to Gwen's apartment, chatting on the way about the brunch and Gwen's plans for the shower. By the time Gwen locked the door behind her, she was full of ideas about the shower and felt confident in her ability to pull it off. She was about to lie down for a nap when there was a knock at the door.

A deliveryman stood on her stoop holding a giant bouquet of pink roses.

"Gwen Marsh?" The kid looked to be about sixteen.

"Yes."

The kid handed her the vase, unceremoniously, then turned around and rushed back to his truck, not even giving Gwen enough time to say thank you. Walking back inside her apartment, she savored the fragrance of the flowers. Pink roses were her favorite. Gwen pulled the card out of its holder. It read *Hey, beautiful!* Smiling, Gwen placed the roses on her coffee table and lay down on the couch to nap, feeling optimistic for the first time in a long time.

* * *

When Jason knocked at Gwen's door later that evening, she felt a little jolt of excitement run through her body. She'd spent the few hours after waking up thinking about what she wanted to say to Jason. She'd decided to say yes to living together, and she hoped he'd be excited.

"Hi!" Gwen threw her arms around Jason's neck, and was rewarded with a long embrace.

"I'm happy to see you, too," he chuckled, leading her into the apartment and closing the door behind him.

"First, thank you for the roses," Gwen said, pointing to the coffee table. "They smell heavenly."

Jason frowned. "They're beautiful. But I didn't send them."

"What?"

"I didn't send them. Was there a card?"

Gwen looked confused, as she muttered distractedly, "But they're my favorites. Who else would send them?" She looked over at Jason, finally acknowledging his question. "There was a card, but no name."

"Val, maybe?"

Gwen picked up her phone and texted her cousin. When her phone buzzed with a response, she frowned. "Nope."

Jason picked up the card and scrutinized it.

"It's not signed, Jason," Gwen said, irritated.

"I know. I wanted to double check." Jason concentrated for a moment. "It has to be someone who knows your favorite flowers. Can't you think of anyone?"

"Maybe it's a coincidence. Pink roses are a pretty popular choice."

For a moment, Jason seemed to relax. Then his frown returned. "No, I don't think so." He started to pace around the living room, deep in thought.

"I don't think we're going to be able to solve the mystery tonight. Why don't we go have some dinner."

"Okay," Jason said, but he still looked frustrated. He stopped at the door. "You know what? I'm feeling pretty tired. Can we skip dinner tonight? I need the rest."

Gwen's face betrayed her surprise. "Sure," she said hesitantly. She felt tears welling up, but she fought to keep them from falling.

Still distracted, Jason kissed her cheek chastely and was out the door without another word.

Gwen sat down on her couch and cried, the scent of roses offering no comfort.

CHAPTER TWENTY-ONE

Gwen walked into City Hall Monday morning feeling depleted, both in body and spirit. After Jason's sudden exit last night, she'd spent a good deal of time crying and staring at the mystery flowers. She didn't understand why they'd upset Jason so much, and not knowing the sender left her feeling uneasy.

Monday mornings were usually fairly relaxed for the mayor. Most meetings were scheduled for other days of the week, so Gwen usually spent her Monday's catching up on correspondence and working on reports.

As she walked past the City Clerk's office, Gwen heard low voices beyond the screen. Was it a coincidence that the talking stopped at the sound of the click of her heels?

Approaching the council office, Gwen's uneasiness turned to full-on anxiety. The door to the office stood wide open, and Gwen saw a small crowd around the worktable. As she got closer, she saw what all the commotion was about. The worktable held another three vases of pink roses, six dozen at least among the lot.

As Gwen stepped across the threshold, Karen Fredrickson, who seemed to be ringleader to the group of gawkers, turned to Gwen and said, "Good morning, Gwen. My, my. You certainly are popular." Karen's smile grew bigger as the color drained from Gwen's face.

"What is all this?" Gwen asked, feeling a little lightheaded.

Karen continued to smirk. "These were delivered for you this morning. Secret admirer? Or is your money man overdoing it as usual?"

The crack about Jason finally brought Gwen to her senses. "If you'll all excuse me, I have work to do." She stood by the door with a grim look on her face. Karen brought up the tail end of the procession.

"Not you. We need to talk," Gwen said, closing the door before Karen had a chance to step out of the office.

"How dare you!" Karen's expression had gone from smug to irate in a matter of seconds. "You don't tell me what to do, Mayor Marsh."

Gwen's patience was long gone. "That's where you're wrong, Karen. The council oversees the city manager's job, and I'm the head of the council. I've had enough of this nonsense. I don't know what I did to offend you, but I will not tolerate another moment of your attempts to undermine and sabotage me." Gwen's breathing was heavy.

"I know you lied to me about the meeting schedule change, and I promise you if that kind of behavior persists, I will file a complaint and move to have you reprimanded."

Karen opened her mouth to speak, but Gwen held up a hand, stopping her in her tracks.

"Until the election, you and I got along fine. We will find a way to do that again. You don't have to like me, Karen, but you will damned well suck it up and do your job. And let me do mine." Finally out of breath, Gwen paused to calm herself down. She was beginning to feel a little bit guilty about her outburst, but one look at the indignant expression on Karen's face erased that feeling.

"You're right, Gwen." Karen started, her voice low and venomous. "I don't like you. You think you're important to this city, but the truth is, you're just a pretty face. I do the real work around here, and what do I get for my trouble? A young, upstart scrutinizing my decisions." The look Karen gave Gwen reminded her of Roger Barton, causing her to shudder.

"We got along so well before," Gwen said, pleadingly. "We were friends."

Karen sneered. "I was never your friend, Gwen. I will tolerate your presence because I know that I'll be here long after you're gone." She stepped past Gwen, opened the door and slammed it behind her.

Gwen leaned back against the door and closed her eyes, focusing on her breathing until it returned to normal. When she'd regained some composure, Gwen walked over to the worktable and studied the roses. Same flowers. Same vases. Same card with the same message. Each vase contained maybe two dozen flowers. Under different circumstances, the sight would have made Gwen smile. It was very romantic. But the fact that someone was sending Gwen an excessive amount of her favorite flowers, both to her home and work, gave her a very queasy feeling.

Gwen sat at her desk, switched on her computer and looked up the number for the florist. She picked up the phone and dialed, ready to get to the bottom of the flower mystery.

"Rocky Mountain Floral."

"Hi, this is Gwen Marsh. A large batch of roses were delivered to City Hall this morning. There's no name on the card. Can you tell me who ordered the flowers?"

"Uh, we're not supposed to give out information about our customers." The employee sounded very young and unsure.

"Do you know who took the order?"

"I did. I'm the only one working up front today. Janie called in sick." To avoid getting all the unnecessary details, Gwen cut the employee off.

"Great, so can I ask a few questions about the person who ordered the flowers?"

There was a pause. "I guess so."

"Was it a man or a woman?"

"It was an online order."

Gwen sighed. "Can I talk to your manager?"

"She's not in right now, but I can have her call you." The voice was getting impatient. Gwen gave the caller her number, and the line was disconnected abruptly. She sat back in her chair and thought about the possibilities. An online order meant it could have come from anywhere. *Obviously someone with money because this many roses had to have cost a small fortune.* Gwen couldn't think of anyone who would send her flowers who she hadn't already ruled out.

Rattled, Gwen tried to focus on some constituent mail, but she couldn't shake the feeling that someone was watching her. She finally broke down and called Val.

"Hey, Gwen." Gwen could hear the click of Val's fingers on her keyboard in the background.

"Are you busy for lunch?"

"No, and I'm already hungry. Want to meet at the deli?"

"Perfect. Usual time?"

"Yep. See you then."

Gwen sat back in her chair and sighed. Someone was trying to make a point. But who? She didn't know whether to feel flattered or afraid. Gwen was not a romantic. While she would have loved flowers from Jason, or Val, or really anyone she knew, this mystery sender left her feeling very unsettled. It was someone who knew her home address. Someone who was brazen enough to send flowers to her office, knowing the gesture would not go unnoticed.

Digging into busy work, the minutes until lunch clicked by so slowly Gwen thought she would go insane. She was relieved when 11 o'clock came around. She practically sprinted out the door of the office, leaving the explosion of pink flowers in her wake.

* * *

The concerned look on Val's face did nothing to put Gwen at ease.

"You have no idea who sent them?" Val asked. She'd been pushing her salad around her plate as Gwen told her the story of the flowers.

"No. And you should have seen Jason's face last night. I don't think he believes me." Gwen had only taken a few bites of her soup, despite the continuous growling in her stomach.

"That's ridiculous. Why would you lie?"

"With everything that's been going on, I think we're both over-sensitive." Gwen scooped up a spoonful of soup, but stopped before putting it in her mouth. "You know, it's weird. I keep seeing Evan around town and now these flowers mysteriously show up. You don't think ...."

"That's a little scary. Do you think you should call the police?"

Gwen shook her head. "And tell them what? That I've seen a person I know around town a few times, and someone sent me some flowers. That's not a crime."

"Not *some* flowers. Hundreds of dollars of flowers, both to your home and office. That's got to count as some kind of harassment."

"Maybe. But I can't be sure it's Evan, and I'd feel terrible if I got him in trouble if it wasn't him."

Val sat silently for a few minutes, still playing with her salad rather than eating it. Gwen took the break in conversation to polish off her bowl of soup. It warmed her up, making her feel much less tense.

"On another strange note," Val began. "Guess who called me the other day?"

"Who?"

"Alfred. You remember, the photographer from the Governor's dinner?"

Gwen raised an eyebrow. "Really? What did he want? I didn't realize you two were still in contact."

Val shrugged. "We aren't. That was the first time I'd heard from him since the election."

"So what did he want?"

"I'm not sure. He wanted to get together, but the whole conversation was really odd, and I put him off."

"For heaven's sake!" Gwen exclaimed, exasperated. "What is going on in this town?"

Val furrowed her brow. "I wouldn't have even mentioned it, but when I thought about who might send you flowers, it occurred to me that if I'd ever suspected anyone of having stalker tendencies, it would be Alfred."

Gwen chuckled. "I guess it's a good thing he's obsessed with you and not me." Val smiled, but the atmosphere remained tense through the rest of their lunch date.

CHAPTER TWENTY-TWO

Jason sat on Gwen's couch, sulking.

"Thank you," Gwen said, shutting the door behind the deliveryman and placing another vase of pink roses on her coffee table. Jason barely glanced at her as she sat down next to him.

"Another delivery from your admirer?" Jason muttered.

Gwen sighed. "I told you, I've tried to figure out who's sending them. I'm going to call tomorrow and refuse further deliveries," she said, then, trying to lighten the mood she added, "Maybe they can take the flowers to the hospital to cheer people up."

Jason grunted and grabbed the remote control to turn on the television, effectively ending the discussion. Gwen moved to the kitchen table to continue working on her to-do list.

To combat her increasing depression, Gwen threw herself into planning Val's bridal shower. Not that there was much to do. Anne Hatfield was nothing if not thorough. An added benefit of working with Anne was her positive attitude about Gwen's pregnancy. Anne never failed to ask Gwen how she felt and to say something sweet about motherhood. For Gwen, the result was a feeling of connection with her baby. Despite all the tension with Jason, she found herself with her hand on her belly, daydreaming about nurseries and baby shoes.

The day before the shower, John's sister June arrived from Seattle. Val and Gwen picked June up from the airport and stopped for lunch.

"What can I do to help with the shower?" June asked after they'd placed their orders.

"Anne wants mimosas tomorrow, and she has a specific type of champagne that she'd like to use. I need to find that today. Otherwise, I think we have everything pretty much under control." Working on the shower plans had been good for Gwen. She was getting really excited about Val's wedding.

"I can pick up the champagne if you'd like me to," June said.

Gwen nodded. "That would be great. I have a meeting this afternoon."

"Mimosas, eh?" Val's nose crinkled.

Gwen giggled. "I know. I told Anne you weren't fond of mimosas, but she said you've never tried *her* mimosas." Gwen winked at Val.

"She's right," June said, smiling. "My mother makes a mimosa like nobody's business. She's always loved a good brunch."

Val was about to respond when her phone buzzed. Looking down at the screen, she frowned.

"What?" Gwen asked, concerned.

"My mom and Liz got in last night for the shower. Mom says something's come up at the hotel, and she needs me to stop by." Val stood. "Gwen, can you box up my lunch? I'll drop by your apartment later."

"Sure," Gwen said, hesitantly. "Is everything okay?"

Val's face relaxed. "I'm sure it is. It's unusual for mom to be so vague." Putting her purse over her shoulder, Val added, "Gwen, can you drop June by Anne's after lunch?"

Gwen smiled. "Of course. I wasn't going to leave her here. Go do what you need to do. I've got you covered."

As Val walked away, the waiter delivered their food. Gwen asked him to box Val's portion. Then she launched into her pasta, suddenly ravenous.

"How are things going, Gwen? You know, personally. If you don't mind me asking."

Gwen smiled. "Given my confession the last time we were together, I'm not surprised by the question. I'm doing pretty well. Feeling much better. I'm finally able to eat, which I seem to do all the time. Still hoping to fit into my bridesmaid's dress." Gwen patted her stomach dramatically.

"I don't think that's going to be a problem," June said, smiling. "You were looking a little skinny the last time I saw you. I'm sure you're back to normal. I'm the one who's got something to worry about."

June was stockier than either Gwen or Val, and she looked like she'd put on a few pounds. Gwen was suddenly embarrassed about her own comments.

"I've formed a new and horrifying relationship with comfort food since moving to Seattle. Missing my 'no-appetite' days."

"Are things getting any better?"

"Yes, actually. I joined a book group at the local bookstore and am finally starting to meet a few people. Even a guy." June winked.

"Ooh, do tell," Gwen said, sounding like a teenager fawning over some juicy gossip.

June chuckled. "Nothing to report. His name is Stephen, and he's a software developer who likes to read romantic comedies. That right there makes him unique. I'm sure there's something terribly wrong with him, but I'll have to do some investigation to find out." June's eyes twinkled with mischief. Gwen only knew a bit about June's personal life, but she remembered Val saying June hadn't done much dating. She'd been primarily focused on her career.

"Actually, I wanted to talk to you about something. I have a problem that I've been reluctant to talk to Val about because I don't want to stress her out before the wedding."

June raised an eyebrow. "Okay, shoot."

"Well," Gwen started, and then paused to gather her thoughts. "I think someone is trying to sabotage my relationship with

Jason, and I also think I have a stalker. I'm not sure the two things are related, but they seem to have sprung up simultaneously, so it's hard not to connect them."

June's brow furrowed. "Let's start with the stalker."

"I worked with a college kid on a voter registration event last month. After the event, he asked me out. I turned him down, and he seemed pretty angry. Now I keep seeing him around town, though I never did before. In fact, he was lurking near the parking lot when we were leaving brunch a few weeks ago."

"Have you approached him?"

"No. At first, I thought I was being paranoid. My emotions have been so crazy lately, I've been prone to overreactions. But it keeps happening, and I really think he's following me. I haven't seen him near my apartment, but definitely around town and City Hall."

"Hmm. So you think he might be trying to break you and Jason up?"

"I don't know. Someone keeps sending me flowers. Huge bouquets of my favorite roses both at home and work. No name on the card, but the messages are flirtatious. The florist can't seem to give me any information about the sender. Just that the orders were made through their website." Gwen paused, thinking, before she continued. "But, I don't see how it could be Evan. He's the college kid. We're talking hundreds of dollars on flowers. I feel like the flowers are coming from someone else, but I can't figure out who."

"Where does Jason fit into this?"

Gwen frowned. "He doesn't believe me when I say I don't know who's sending them. He's been really distant and cranky. I get the feeling that's what the person sending the flowers is after. Otherwise, why not sign the card?"

June thought for a moment. "So, two things. First, call the florist, and stop all future deliveries."

"Done."

"Good. Second, I think you need to confront Evan, preferably with the help of the police. If he's simply some kid with a crush, the police attention will stop that behavior right away. But if he's dangerous, you want the police alerted."

Gwen's heart began to race. "I can't believe Evan is dangerous," she said, though she began to feel a little sick with anxiety.

"Have you told Jason about Evan?"

Gwen hesitated. "No. Jason's already so grumpy with me, I didn't want to fuel his suspicions."

June was quiet for a few minutes, which made Gwen nervous. "When is your meeting this afternoon?"

"Not until four o'clock. Why?"

"Let's address the stalking. I'll go with you, and we'll figure out what to do next."

"Oh, June. You don't have to. I feel embarrassed even telling you about this." Gwen's face was red with emotion.

June smiled. "No, you were right to tell me. Let's take care of it so you can spend your time worrying about more important things. Like wedding showers and bridesmaid's dresses."

Gwen still felt embarrassed, but she also felt relieved. She'd only mentioned Evan's behavior to Victoria but downplayed it in case she'd made too much out of it. She hadn't realized how tense she felt until she talked it through with June.

Gwen paid for lunch, and the two women headed downtown to the police station. The officer she spoke with gave her instructions for recording Evan's appearances, flower deliveries, and any other actions that might be considered harassment. He explained they needed documentation before contacting Evan, but if she ever felt she was in danger, she should call 911. With her report on record, Gwen felt a bit more in control of her situation and ready to face whatever came next.

Gwen dropped June at Anne's house and headed home for a nap. She walked into her afternoon meeting with a renewed jolt of confidence.

* * *

Jason picked Gwen up for dinner. He'd arrived home a few hours earlier. Gwen had been tied up with work, so Jason found himself with a few free hours and a mind full of worry.

Jason's team was assigned to the Denver office for the next few weeks. Under normal circumstances, Jason would have been relieved to have some time at home, to see Gwen every night and to recover from all the travel he'd been doing lately. But having Alex in Denver was going to be a problem.

The biggest issue was that Jason and Gwen were on very shaky ground at the moment. Jason admitted it was mostly his fault. He'd reacted very badly to the flowers Gwen kept receiving. He believed she didn't know who the sender was, but it didn't stop him from feeling incredibly jealous and irritated. Gwen had never given Jason a reason not to trust her, but there was so much about her life he didn't know. He realized when she broke the news about her relationship with her parents. Here they were, having a baby together, and there were huge parts of her life that he had no clue about. So Jason withdrew. It didn't help, but he was at a loss for what to do differently.

He knew that part of his overreaction to the flowers came from his own sense of guilt. Jason suspected Alex was interested in him romantically. He'd tried hard to write Alex's goodnight kiss off as a friendly gesture, but it was no use. Her coy smiles and flirtatious behavior did not reflect platonic intentions.

Over the last few weeks, Alex found ways to talk Jason into spending more time with her. The restaurants she chose were more romantic: dim lights, flowers, soft music. Anytime Jason questioned her choice, Alex would shrug innocently and change the subject.

Jason wasn't helping the situation. He spoke so infrequently about Gwen that it was like she didn't exist. He hadn't told a soul about the pregnancy, waiting until he and Gwen were on surer ground before breaking the news. He admitted he found

Alex very attractive. She was fun to be with, and, more than once, he'd found himself focused on the nape of her neck, the curve of her hips.

Keeping things professional was becoming an issue, causing Jason to panic. He'd hoped that the stint in Denver would allow him to reclaim some normalcy, but that dream had been dashed. Earlier in the day, Alex made a point of coming to find him.

"Hey, stranger. I missed you at happy hour last night." A group of co-workers met up for drinks after work the previous day, and Jason purposefully avoided the gathering, hoping to put some much-needed distance between himself and Alex.

"I needed a night in. Too much going on lately. I'm looking forward to being home and sleeping in my own bed."

"That's what I wanted to talk to you about," Alex said, a slight blush creeping onto her cheeks. "Since we're going to be in Denver for a few weeks, I wondered if you'd introduce me to Gwen. Maybe show me around town." The hopeful look on Alex's face made Jason's adverse reaction seem all the more wrong.

"Um. I'm sure that would be okay. Let's touch base next week," he hedged, when Alex interrupted.

"Actually, you've made Cambria sound so nice that I booked a hotel there. I thought maybe we could drive into work together." Alex's look was all innocence, but the twinkle in her eye made Jason nervous.

"Oh. I guess that makes sense. When are you getting to town?"

"Not until Sunday late. I have to go take care of a few things at home before I leave. But if you don't mind taking your car to Denver, I'll take the train to the hotel."

"Okay," Jason said, his voice strained.

"Are you sure it's alright?" Alex asked.

"It's fine," Jason insisted. But it wasn't.

It irritated Jason, the way Alex assumed she could schedule his time. He realized he could always tell her no, but the way she presented things made him feel like a jerk turning her down. Unfortunately, he was beginning to suspect she knew it.

Jason brooded as he and Gwen headed out to dinner. In fact, they didn't speak at all until they were seated at their table in the restaurant.

"How was your week?" Jason said, hoping to keep the attention on Gwen until he figured out what to do.

"It was pretty good. Busy. June got in today. Actually, I need to talk to you about something." Gwen's look of determination made Jason smile despite his tension. He loved that look. "I went to the police today."

"You what?" Jason was instantly on high alert. "What happened?"

"I think this college kid I worked with on the voter registration event—Evan—I think he's been following me around. He asked me out after the event and seemed pretty angry when I said no. Now he keeps popping up when I'm out and about."

"How long has this been going on?" Jason said, through gritted teeth.

"A little over a month."

"Is he sending the flowers?"

"I don't know. I don't think so. I don't see how he could afford all those flowers. But I do think someone is trying to interfere in our relationship. Anyway, I called the florist and blocked all future deliveries." Gwen looked into Jason's eyes. "So don't send me any flowers, okay?" she said, smiling, hoping to lighten the mood.

"When were you going to tell me about this?" Jason said. His face turned red, and she saw a vein pulsing in his forehead.

Gwen looked down. "I didn't want to tell you at all. You've been so moody lately, and every time I bring up the flowers, you get mad. I didn't want to fight about it." When she turned her eyes up to Jason, they were filled with tears. Jason's anger softened a bit.

"It's frustrating, Gwen. When you found out you were pregnant, you didn't tell me right away. Now you've waited weeks to bring this up. It makes me wonder what else you're keeping from me." Seeing the instant hurt in Gwen's eyes, Jason wished he could take the comment back.

Their food was delivered, and they ate in silence. Gwen looked out the window, around the restaurant, anywhere but Jason. Feeling extremely guilty, Jason finally spoke up.

"I'm sorry, Gwen. I didn't mean that."

After a few more minutes of silence, Gwen looked at Jason. "No, you're kind of right. Having you away from home so much is making things really hard right now. We spend so little time together, I don't want to make it more stressful than it already has been."

"You've got a lot going on." Jason thought for a few minutes. "I wish I had never taken this job," he said, more to himself than to Gwen.

"You like the job, right?" Gwen asked.

"Yes. But if I had known about the baby, I never would have applied. Being away from you makes me feel like I'm not part of it."

Jason took Gwen's hand across the table, and they sat quietly for a few minutes.

"I'll be in the Denver office until after the wedding, so maybe we can make up for some lost time." Jason smiled, warmly.

"That would be wonderful. You'll have some flexibility in when you go into the office, right?"

The warm feeling left Jason immediately. "Not exactly. Alex asked if she could ride into work with me so she doesn't have to rent a car."

Gwen's face turned stony. "She's not staying in Denver?"

Jason felt the color creeping into his face. "No. She's staying in Cambria. She asked to meet you and wanted to know if we would show her around town."

"I'm sure that'll be fine."

Jason knew that it wasn't.

"I have Val's bridal shower tomorrow and then more wedding work to do next weekend."

"I should have told her no." Jason said, hoping to turn the tide of the conversation, but the damage was already done.

Gwen put on her "public" face and said, "No, no. It's fine. You're both going to work in Denver. No reason not to go together." The forced cheerfulness in her voice hit Jason like a sledgehammer. This was going to be bad.

CHAPTER TWENTY-THREE

Determined not to let her stress ruin Val's shower, Gwen arrived at Anne's house early and helped set up with a vengeance. She smiled, she chatted, she decorated, but inside she felt like screaming. The mere mention of Alex's name was enough to raise her pulse. Gwen couldn't help but notice that Jason was a lot less moody on the phone than in town. She'd assumed his mood was mostly based on their relationship troubles, but now she wasn't so sure.

"Gwen?" Val said. Gwen hadn't seen her approach.

"Hmm?" she murmured. Pulled back into the moment, she gave Val a big hug. "Sorry, just thinking."

"Everything looks beautiful." Val scanned the patio, which had been completely transformed with autumn-colored flowers.

Gwen grinned, her thoughts temporarily shifted from her own problems. "Your mother-in-law-to-be is really something. When she goes all out, she really goes all out."

Val nodded. "Yes. But I hope she doesn't think I'll be able to follow in her footsteps. I can't even imagine pulling off this shower, much less a whole wedding." Val took Gwen's arm. "Can we sit down for a few minutes? I need to talk to you."

"Okay," Gwen said, setting down the napkin she'd been folding.

The cousins walked back into the house and found a quiet corner in the parlor.

"How are things going with Jason?" Val asked.

Wondering what she'd heard, Gwen cringed. She'd been very reluctant to share all the details of her disastrous relationship with Val so close to her wedding. "We're okay. Still trying to get on the same page." But Gwen's tone was not convincing, even to herself. And Val knew her too well not to have noticed.

"What's going on?" Val asked, concern showing in her eyes. "Jason called John last night, and I gather he was upset. John didn't tell me what they talked about, but it seemed tense."

"We had a pretty rough night. I sent him home early, right after dinner." Still reluctant to elaborate, Gwen let her words fall away. But Val would not be deterred.

"What happened?"

Gwen sighed, seeing there was no way out of coming clean. "You know he'll be in Denver the next two weeks, right? His co-worker Alex has decided to stay in Cambria, and she wants to ride to work with him every day."

Val pursed her lips, but stayed quiet, allowing Gwen to continue.

"Apparently, she wants to meet me."

"Really?" Val's tone betrayed a hint of suspicion, which made Gwen feel a little less crazy.

"I know. Jason says they're friends, and I guess it would be normal for friends to want to get to know each other's families, right?" Gwen didn't sound convinced.

"I suppose. But it's strange she decided to stay in Cambria." Val thought for a few moments then sighed. "I'm sure it's fine, Gwen. When John and Jason hung out a few weeks ago, Jason made it clear he's committed to you and the baby." Val couldn't help herself. She patted Gwen's stomach and giggled.

"Cut it out! I don't need everyone at your party to know." Gwen gave Val's shoulder a squeeze. "Enough talk about me. Things can't get a whole lot worse, so let's leave it for today. Today is about you and John!"

"One more thing unfortunately." The look on Val's face

made Gwen uneasy. "I need to talk to you about my mom's call yesterday."

"I totally forgot! What's going on?"

"Well," Val started, but she seemed hesitant to go forward. Then, before she could continue, her eyes grew wider. Gwen turned in time to see Val's mom and her sister Liz walk through the door, followed by Gwen's mother, Leann.

"Oh, shit," Gwen said, overtaken by the sudden urge to leave. "Why is she here?"

Val sighed. "She showed up at mom's hotel room yesterday. Apparently, she's decided to come to the shower. And the wedding."

"You invited her?" Gwen couldn't help the accusatory tone, though she felt guilty.

"It wasn't my idea. Anne insisted on inviting the whole family. You know, etiquette and all. I never thought she'd actually come. I haven't seen her since dad's funeral, and that was bad enough." Ever the drama queen, Leann made a scene at the funeral, leaving a bad taste in Val's mouth.

As the group made their way into the foyer, Gwen's eyes found her mother's. Leann broke away from the group and strode dramatically to Gwen, arms outstretched.

"Gwennie! Oh, my baby. It's so good to see you!" Leann's voice was loud enough to echo through the house. "Darling, you look like you've put on weight." Leann's smile gave Gwen a vision of a predator hunting her prey.

"Hello, Mom. What brings you to Cambria?" Gwen's tone was biting.

"There's no need to be impolite, Gwen. I'm here to see my favorite niece get married." She stole a quick glance at Val. "And to see my only child, of course."

"The wedding isn't for two weeks. You're coming back?" Gwen asked, her curiosity piqued.

"Of course not. I'm staying with you."

Gwen looked at Val, who grimaced. "I live in a tiny apartment with one bed, Mom. Where are you going to sleep?"

"Can't you give up your bed for you dear old Mom?" Leann batted her eyelashes, making Gwen instantly furious.

"Not for two weeks. I need my sleep too. Can't you stay in a hotel?"

Leann's face dropped. "I suppose so, but I *had* hoped we could catch up. You know, spend some good old mother-daughter time."

A hateful retort was on Gwen's lips, but by some miracle, Val's mom approached at that moment and took Leann's arm. "Come on, Leann. I want to introduce you to John's sister, June." She tugged Leann away, chatting the entire time.

Val put her arm around Gwen's shoulder. "Breathe."

"This is all I need. Alex in Cambria. My mother in Cambria. What did I do to deserve this?" Gwen sighed and leaned into Val. She allowed herself a few minutes to pout and then straightened up. "Alright, enough feeling sorry for myself. Sweet cousin, let's go celebrate your impending nuptials to the scrumptious John Hatfield." Gwen gave Val a coy look. The two linked arms and headed to the patio.

* * *

The week following Val's shower was like navigating a minefield. Gwen's mom became a frequent fixture at Gwen's apartment, despite booking a hotel room. Gwen, who wasn't about to tell her mother about the pregnancy, had to modify her routines to ensure she got enough sleep, as her ability to nap throughout the day had been interrupted.

Gwen worked hard to keep Leann at arm's length, since it was her mother's propensity to insert herself anywhere she sensed drama or tension. She managed to keep Leann and Jason from meeting each other for several days, but her luck ran out. By Friday night, she'd run out of excuses for not introducing them.

"Okay, Mom. We'll all go out to dinner tonight," Gwen said gruffly into her phone. "I'll call you later with the details."

She spent the afternoon at City Hall to avoid another day with her mother breathing down her neck. A quick glance at the clock told her she only had a few more hours of peace.

The irony that City Hall had become a refuge was not lost on Gwen. Since she confronted Karen Fredrickson, the working environment had become less hostile, though their interactions remained cold and impersonal. Gwen's mother, who'd apparently developed a distaste for the government through the years, avoided City Hall, making it the ideal escape.

Jason stayed over at Gwen's apartment most of the week, appearing on her doorstep late in the evenings. Instead of enjoying a week of togetherness, their meetings felt clandestine, and more than once Gwen felt like the other woman. Jason tried not to talk about work at all, and it was obvious he was not going to mention Alex in front of Gwen unless absolutely necessary.

Gwen's phone buzzed.

"Hey, I wanted to let you know I'm home early." Jason sounded tired.

"I told my mom we'd have dinner tonight," Gwen said, without enthusiasm.

"You sure you're ready for this?" Jason had been privy to long rants about Gwen's mother during the week. Gwen was still suspicious about why Leann was in town, and in the meantime, her "loving mother" act began to wear on Gwen.

"No. But I can't see any way out of it. She'll be here another week, and I'd rather not have to deal with her meeting you at the wedding. Too much drama."

"Okay. Should I pick you up?"

"That would be great. I walked into work today. Needed some fresh air. Can you swing by around five?" Gwen looked up at the clock on the wall and wondered what she would do for another two hours. Returning home was out of the question.

"Sure. Err, Gwen?" The tone in Jason's voice had Gwen on

high alert. "Alex asked if we could get together tomorrow for lunch and then some sightseeing."

Gwen worked hard not to let her irritation creep into her voice. "I can do lunch, but then I'm due at Anne's for some last-minute wedding prep."

"I'll tell her no on the sightseeing then."

Without thinking, Gwen said, "No, why don't you just take her. I'm going to be busy all afternoon. There's no point in you canceling." Of course, the minute she said it, she wished she hadn't. The thought of Jason and Alex alone together was irksome.

Jason hesitated. "Are you sure?"

Gwen's temper flared, but she kept her tone in check. "Yes." She paused for a deep breath. "I need to go. I'll see you in a bit." She disconnected quickly, relieved to be off the phone. Gwen was annoyed with herself. She wasn't the type of woman who played games. Yet, a part of her hoped Jason would sense her discomfort and decide to cancel his plans with Alex. No such luck.

They're just friends. They're just friends. They're just friends. Gwen chanted this mantra while trying to slow her breathing and relax. It was Friday afternoon, and City Hall was especially quiet. In another hour, most of the staff would be gone. Gwen finished all her work for the week, and there was nothing much left to do. She'd been thinking about taking a walk, but the anticipation of dinner with her mother followed by lunch with Alex made her want to avoid people for a while. She needed to get herself to a better mental place so she could tolerate the weekend ahead.

Gwen made herself a cup of hot tea and returned to her laptop. She did her city work on a government computer, but always brought her laptop for personal work and correspondence. She pulled up her Internet browser and navigated to Google. She'd intended to do some online shopping, but found herself entering "Alexandra Barnes" into the search bar.

This is ridiculous, Gwen thought, but she hit enter and watched as the search results loaded. Scrolling through the search results, she noticed a link to a LinkedIn profile with BGB listed as the current job. Gwen clicked the link and waited while Alex's profile loaded. The picture was clearly a professional head shot, but despite its formality, Gwen couldn't help but notice Alex was very beautiful. Her wavy hair lay flawlessly on her shoulder, framing delicate features and dazzling green eyes.

Looking at those eyes made Gwen queasy. *Of course he's attracted to her,* she thought. Gwen scanned Alex's professional and educational background. She noticed that Alex seemed to change jobs every two years, sometimes more frequently. *Maybe that's normal for her job.*

Alex's profile revealed an accomplished woman with volunteer service in some of the same areas as Gwen. *We could be friends,* Gwen thought, though she knew how ridiculous this thought was. She hadn't even met Alex, and she already disliked her intensely. Gwen spent a few more minutes reading the recommendations former colleagues left for Alex. Then she closed the window and rested her heads in her hands.

She must have started to doze, because the next thing she knew, someone shook her shoulder gently, causing her to jump.

"Gwen?" Jason stood behind Gwen, who'd apparently been sleeping with her head on the desk in front of her. "Gwen? Are you alright?"

Gwen yawned. "I'm okay. I must have dozed off. It's been so quiet all afternoon."

"Yeah, there's no one around. When you didn't answer my text, I decided to park and come in." Jason chuckled. "Guess it's a good thing I did." Jason wore his cornflower blue shirt, Gwen's favorite, and she smelled his aftershave, one of her favorite scents. She sat up and stretched.

"You look handsome," Gwen said, gazing sleepily up at Jason. Still dazed from her unexpected nap, she was overcome by feelings of tenderness for Jason. Unfortunately, the feelings were short-lived, as she remembered their task for the evening. Gwen sighed. "I told mom we'd pick her up at her hotel at six. I want to go home and change."

Jason nodded, and walked Gwen to his car. Thirty minutes later, Gwen had changed into her favorite blue dress, and she and Jason were on their way to Leann's hotel. Jason seemed more agitated as they approached the hotel.

"She's not answering her phone," Gwen said, frustrated. "Let's park, and we'll walk up to get her."

Jason sighed, but didn't say anything as he found a parking space near the front entrance. As they walked in the lobby, Jason laced his fingers with Gwen's. As they rounded the corner toward the elevators, Gwen felt someone approaching from the side. She turned and came face to face with Alex Barnes.

"Hi Jason!" Alex said excitedly. "What a nice surprise." Her eyes then traveled to Gwen, pausing for a moment on their intertwined hands. "You must be Gwen." Alex stuck out her hand enthusiastically, but there was something in her expression that made Gwen feel nervous.

"Alex, this is my girlfriend, Gwen Marsh," Jason said, shortly. "Gwen, this is my co-worker Alex Barnes."

The women shook hands quickly.

"What brings you two here?" Alex asked, sweetly.

"My mother is staying here, too. We're picking her up for dinner." Gwen looked past Alex in time to see Leann step off the elevators. Seeing Gwen, she walked quickly to join the small group.

"Hello, Gwen!" Leann scanned the tense group, and Gwen saw a sparkle in her eye. Leann loved her drama.

Leaning in to give her a quick hug, Gwen said, "Mom, this is Jason. Jason, my mother Leann." Leann gave a Jason a hug, leaving him a little startled. "And this is Alex Barnes. She works with Jason."

Leann gave Alex an appraising look. "You don't live in the area?"

"No, I live in Salt Lake City. I'm a project manager with BGB's western division so Jason and I do a lot of traveling together." Alex smiled, but the wording of her answer annoyed Gwen.

Jason interjected, "We're responsible for four sites in the region so our team does a lot of site visits." He emphasized the word "team" clumsily, making Gwen cringe.

"I see," Leann said, but Gwen saw the wheels in her head spinning. "Will you be joining us for dinner, Alex?" she continued, smiling coyly at Gwen.

"Oh, no. I've got plans, but thank you for thinking of me." Alex said goodbye and headed out the lobby doors to a waiting taxi.

The remaining three stood in silence for a few moments, watching the taxi pull away from the curb. Hoping to head off any further discussion of Alex, Gwen said abruptly, "Shall we go? I'm starving."

CHAPTER TWENTY-FOUR

Alex certainly is lovely," Leann said the moment they sat down at their table.

Jason buried his nose in his menu, leaving Gwen to interact with her mother. "Yes, she is. She's been a good friend to Jason." Sticking up for Alex left a bad taste in Gwen's mouth, but her distaste for her mother was far more pressing.

Looking amused, Leann turned her attention to Jason. "So, Jason. What looks good?"

"I like the chicken piccata. The sauce here is delicious."

The rest of the night was an intricate dance. Leann would bring up Alex. Jason and Gwen would sidestep the conversation, changing the subject or giving short answers that left no room for further discussion.

Even more frustrating was Leann's foray into the topic of marriage.

"You've been dating for a year, right? When're you going to get married?" She batted her eyelashes innocently.

Jason's face turned beet red. Gwen decided she'd had enough. "You know what, Mom. We'd rather not talk about our personal lives."

Leann smirked. "I'm your mother, Gwen. Why wouldn't we talk about personal things?"

"You're going to have to spend more than a few days playing mother before I feel like opening up to you." Gwen's teeth were gritted as she waited for Leann's response. Luckily, the food arrived, and all three dug in. Each time Leann began another attempt at interrogation, Gwen deflected by answering with questions or commenting on the food. The drive home was tense, and Jason heaved a huge sigh of relief when they dropped Leann back at her hotel.

Looking at Gwen, he said. "I think I see what you mean about Leann."

Gwen sat back in her seat and took a deep breath. *Just a few more days and she'll go away again.*

***

No matter how hard she tried, Gwen couldn't relax. She watched Jason as he drove toward Alex's hotel. His face was hard and tense.

"Hey," she patted his arm. "Are you alright?"

Jason's muscles relaxed. "After last night, I'm not looking forward to another tense meal."

"I know what you mean. If I could have gotten out of dinner with my mom, I would have. Believe me." She smiled, reassuringly. "But this lunch should be okay." Her heart wasn't in her words, and she was pretty sure Jason could tell.

"Nothing like hanging out with co-workers on your day off." Gwen raised a brow in Jason's direction, but his mind was completely focused on the road.

When they arrived at the hotel, Alex waited on the curb. She wore a UCLA sweatshirt over ragged looking jeans. *At least she's not trying too hard*, Gwen thought with a smile.

Alex climbed in the back seat behind Gwen. "Hi guys. What's on the agenda?" She seemed very relaxed. For a moment, Gwen felt silly for feeling jealous. "You weren't kidding about Cambria being beautiful. I could stay here forever." *Nope*, thought Gwen, feeling that familiar tug in her stomach.

They made their way to Jose's, one of Gwen's favorite Mexican restaurants. Her mouth began to water as they approached.

"Mexican! My favorite!" Alex squealed. "You remembered, Jason."

Gwen could feel the heat in her cheeks. She looked out the window, waiting for her color to return to normal.

"Gwen's too." There was panic in Jason's voice.

They walked inside and were escorted to a booth near the window. Jason directed Gwen to one side, and then scooted in close beside her. Alex didn't appear flustered. She looked around the restaurant, taking it all in.

"This place is beautiful. Like that last place we ate at in Arizona."

Jason cringed. "But Colorado Mexican food is different than Arizona, so keep an open mind." He turned to Gwen. "What's that plate you usually order, babe?"

"The tacos al pastor. They're marinated and topped in pineapple." Gwen studied Alex closely.

Alex smiled. "That sounds wonderful. What are you having, Jason?"

Jason shifted uncomfortably in his seat. "I think the burrito supreme. The green chile sauce is really good here."

"Ooh, I think I'll get that too."

Is she seriously goading me? Gwen tried to give Alex the benefit of the doubt, but everything about the girl irked Gwen. Her smile seemed too wide to be genuine, and she was too perky.

"How have you been enjoying your job at BGB, Alex?" Gwen asked. She noticed Jason was arranging his silverware and avoiding eye contact with either woman.

"It's been great! The learning curve is steep, but luckily I've got some great co-workers. Don't you think so, Jason?" Alex winked in Jason's direction.

"Everyone is very helpful." Jason's discomfort was plain to see.

"Jason tells me you're the mayor here in Cambria?" Alex smiled sweetly, making Gwen's stomach curl.

"Yes. I've been in office almost a year now. It certainly keeps me busy."

"I can imagine. It must be a relief to have Jason out of the way," Alex paused awkwardly before adding, "So you can work on your career."

Gwen was losing patience. "Oh, we've done a pretty good job of staying connected. Don't you think, sweetie?" Gwen laced her fingers through Jason's, making sure their hands were fully visible. Jason looked like he wanted to disappear.

The rest of lunch was spent in forced but polite conversation. After lunch, Jason gave Gwen a ride back to her apartment so she could get her car and head to Anne's house for Val's shower. When they arrived, Gwen leaned over to kiss Jason on the cheek. As she exited the car, Alex jumped out the back seat and nudged past Gwen to climb into the passenger seat beside Jason. Before she sat down, she turned to Gwen and said, "Don't worry. I'll take good care of him."

***

"So, what did you think of Leann?" John asked Jason. It was the night before the wedding. Instead of a traditional stag party, which John insisted would be traumatic, Jason arranged for him, John, and John's brother David to hang out at their favorite sports bar. David hadn't arrived yet, so John took the opportunity to catch up with Jason.

Jason shrugged. "She's a piece of work. I'm not sure what to make of her. She's playing the doting mother, but from what Gwen tells me, this is very unusual behavior."

"Val said Gwen has had it with this visit." John smiled. "Have you guys told her about the baby yet?"

"No. Gwen doesn't want her to know, especially right now before the wedding. Apparently, Leann likes to make a scene, and Gwen doesn't want to give her any fodder."

"I can understand that. You guys shouldn't tell people until you're both ready."

Jason fidgeted with his napkin, until he finally noticed John staring.

Amy Rivers

"What's going on?" John asked. "You've been weird all day."

Jason hesitated. He'd wanted to avoid talking about his problems and keep the focus on John, but now that they were sitting across from each other, Jason wanted desperately to spill his guts.

"It turns out my co-worker Alex is staying at the same hotel as Leann. We ran into Alex when we were picking Leann up for dinner. Now it seems that Leann has made it her business to seek Alex out and befriend her."

"I bet Gwen is loving that," John said, his voice dripping with sarcasm.

"It's pretty much a disaster. Gwen and I had lunch with Alex on Saturday, and there was some serious posturing."

"Why?"

"I think Gwen is jealous. She looks jealous." Jason paused. "And I think Alex is interested in me after all."

John frowned. "I wondered. But she clearly knows you're with Gwen, right?"

"Yes, and she's going out of her way to be nice to Gwen, but even I can see it's a competition." Jason sighed miserably, taking a drink from his beer mug.

John looked at Jason seriously. "And your feelings for Alex?"

Jason let out another big sigh. "I admit, I find her attractive. But these past two weeks having her here in Cambria has been a nightmare. It's probably a good thing it happened actually, because any stupid notions I had about Alex are gone. I just want her to go away."

"At least now that you've made up your mind it'll be easier to keep things professional."

"I don't know," Jason said nervously. "Alex doesn't take no for an answer. She pops up in my office and announces our lunch plans. And when I try to say no, she pouts, and I feel guilty."

John frowned again. "You're heading for trouble, man."

"Don't I know it." Jason took another drink of his beer.

"Something's going to have to give. I have to go back to California next week, and I'm dreading it."

John was about to respond when David approached the booth. He swung in next to John and ordered a beer.

"Walked into a heavy conversation, huh?" David said, seeing the tense look on Jason's face.

"Hey, David. It's good to see you." Jason tried to perk up a bit. "We were talking about Gwen."

"Ah, the young mayor." David winked. "How's Ms. Marsh doing these days?"

"Perpetually stressed out," Jason smiled. "There's been a lot of drama at work. And her mother came out of the woodwork for John's wedding so she's got drama at home as well."

David chuckled. "Yes, I met the intrepid Leann Marsh yesterday."

"Really?" John asked.

"I took Mother to dinner last night, and we ran into Leann. She made a beeline for our table like we were long lost family." David's beer arrived, and he took a big swig before continuing. "She was with this gorgeous brunette. Did she bring someone with her?"

Jason gulped. "No, that would be Alex. She works with me at BGB."

The curiosity on David's face was unmistakable. "Oh, this sounds interesting."

Jason frowned. "Not so much interesting as a total disaster." Reluctantly, he filled David in on the details of his relationship with Alex.

"Whoa, you're neck deep in drama." David gave Jason a sympathetic look. "I hate to tell you this, but those two were thick as thieves the entire night. They were seated a few tables away and kept glancing over at us."

Jason sighed. "I'm sorry, John. This is the worst stag party ever."

John smiled. "I disagree. I had this horrible vision of a room full of drunken fools drooling over a stripper. This is much more tolerable."

Jason laughed, feeling a little better. "Not really your style, eh?"

"Definitely not." John raised his glass. "To Jason, for knowing me well enough not to hire a stripper!"

Glass in the air, David added, "And to John, for having the good sense to marry Val and, therefore, transcend all this adolescent crap the rest of us have to deal with."

"Hear, hear," Jason said, grinning.

***

As she walked down the aisle clutching her elegant bouquet, Gwen couldn't help but imagine herself as the bride, walking toward a smiling Jason. Of course, this wasn't her wedding. It was Val's. She walked toward the altar where a smiling John looked happier than she'd ever seen him. Next to him, Jason looked at Gwen with such love that it was impossible not to feel warmth pulsing through her body.

After the bachelor party, Jason showed up at Gwen's, looking lower than she'd ever seen him. He barely spoken a word the whole night, but he kept her close, cuddling her like he couldn't bear the thought of being physically apart. It reminded her of the first days of their relationship, and Gwen realized the last few months had been absurd. Jason was the man she loved, the father of her child, and whatever it took to make things right between them, she was determined to see it happen.

Gwen looked down at her dress as she made her way down the aisle, her royal blue gown caught the light, making it shimmer. She felt beautiful, which, given the week she'd had, was a miracle. With her mother skulking around and Alex demanding Jason's attention, Gwen had started to feel like a mushroom, hiding in the shadows of her own life.

Gwen took her place beside June and watched as Val floated down the aisle. Val was radiant, her dark hair cascading down bare shoulders. She'd chosen a dazzling strapless wedding gown with sparkling crystal embellishments everywhere. Gwen was surprised to see Val in such a lavish gown, Val being her simple, no-nonsense cousin. The look on John's face as Val walked toward him was priceless.

Before taking her place next to John, Val winked at Gwen. Despite months of worry, the wedding was beautiful. Right up until the last moment, Val had gone through her mental check-list, spending way too much time on all the things that could go wrong. But as Gwen predicted, Anne's planning was flawless, her taste impeccable. As long as they all played their roles, everything would go off without a hitch. Even Leann seemed subdued, as if wanting to impress Anne by behaving like a normal human being.

As the ceremony commenced, Gwen found herself reflecting on her relationship with Val. They had grown up together, like sisters. Over the years, there had been gaps in their relationship. When Gwen was away at college, she and Val hardly saw each other. But when she'd moved back to Cambria, Gwen and Val picked up right where they left off.

In the past few months, Gwen suffered from frequent bouts of envy over how easily Val's love life had fallen into place. When they'd started dating, Gwen hadn't held out much hope for Val and John. They'd both been awkward, shy and inexperienced in matters of the heart. Never a romantic, Gwen wasn't drawn to the notion of "happily ever after" the way some women were. But John had become Val's knight in shining armor, coaxing her out of her shell, bringing out the best in her.

Now, standing here, celebrating the first moments of their new life together, Gwen realized her love for Val and John transcended any jealousy she'd felt. She looked up at Jason; his eyes were glistening with tears. Their eyes met, and he smiled.

"Do you take this woman to be your wife?"

Gwen looked deep into Jason's eyes and knew what her own answer would be.

"I do." Val's voice spoke Gwen's heart.

The ceremony ended in a kiss, and Mr. and Mrs. John Hatfield joined hands and walked back down the aisle to the joyful applause of their guests. Gwen walked toward Jason, took his hand and followed John and Val to their places in the receiving line. Before the guests converged on the bride and groom, Gwen turned to her cousin.

"Congratulations, Val," she said, dabbing away at the tears flowing unimpeded down her cheeks. "I love you so much, and I am so happy for you."

Stepping beside Gwen, Jason added, "You look stunning, Val."

John stepped closer to Val. "Yes, you do. I love you, beautiful wife."

Val looked into John's eyes, blushing. "Love you, too, handsome husband." Then Val turned to Gwen and Jason. "We love you both. Take care of each other."

Gwen felt Jason take her hand in his again. "I love you, Gwen," he whispered in her ear.

The rest of the evening was a blissful blur. Gwen danced until she thought her heart was going to burst. Val's mom managed to keep Leann at bay, giving Gwen the space to enjoy herself. She was able to put all her worries aside for the evening. She clung to Jason during the slow songs, savoring the smell of his cologne and the beat of his heart as she rested her head on his chest. For the first time in months, everything seemed right.

CHAPTER TWENTY-FIVE

Sunday morning, Gwen slept in late, snuggling deeper into the covers every time the urge to get out of bed struck her. Jason got up a little earlier to make some tea, but he'd fallen back asleep and snored lightly beside Gwen. When they'd gotten home from the reception last night, Gwen switched off her phone and left it out on the kitchen table for good measure, still feeling blissfully happy and unwilling to allow any interruptions from the outside world.

They'd made love for the first time in weeks. Slowly, then passionately, as if rediscovering each other. Gwen rolled toward Jason, resting her head on his shoulder, basking in the memories.

"Good morning," he said, sleepily running his fingers through her hair. His eyes were still closed, but he smiled. "I made you some tea, but then I fell asleep."

Gwen smiled. "I know. I couldn't make myself get out of bed to have some. I can't remember the last time I felt this relaxed."

"Me too." He wrapped his arms around her. "Let's stay like this all day."

Gwen giggled. "I wish. I told mom I'd meet her for lunch. I think she's planning on leaving today."

"Gwen, before we get out of bed or have to deal with the real world, can I ask you something?"

"Sure."

"Do you love me?"

Gwen crinkled her nose, thinking Jason was joking, but one look at his face told her he was serious. She took a breath, knowing the drama of the last few months rendered her knee-jerk response unacceptable. She owed Jason some honesty.

"I do, very much. At the wedding, I realized how ridiculous I've been the last few months. The truth is, I'm scared. Scared of having this baby. Scared of committing. And mostly, scared of losing you." Gwen paused, but Jason lay silently, listening. "I never thought of myself as a traditional woman, the kind who gets married and has children. It's not that I don't want those things, but all the things that have happened to me in my life have driven home the idea that I have to take care of myself."

"It's funny. Isn't that how Val was too? Before John?"

"Yes. I've even given her a hard time about it. Talk about hypocritical. But then, sometimes it's easier to give advice then to take it." Gwen grinned. "My dad left when I was two years old. I've never had a relationship with him beyond the occasional birthday card or call. When you talk about moving in together, all I can picture is how painful it will be when you leave me."

Jason sighed. "I can understand that. Now, anyway. I wish I'd known how you were feeling a long time ago. Maybe I wouldn't have been so hurt by your refusals."

"I know. I should have told you these things before. I hadn't realized the kind of control issues I have until I found out I was pregnant. Talk about life giving me a good dose of reality." Gwen shifted up on one elbow and looked down at Jason. "Jason, I do love you. So much. I'm sorry I've behaved so badly."

Jason rested his hand on her cheek, staring into her eyes. "I'm sorry too, Gwen. I feel like I've made all the wrong decisions, all the wrong moves, ever since I quit my job at the city."

Gwen rested back on her pillow, and they lay silently for a while.

"Gwen?"

"Mm hmm?"

"I want us to live together. I know things are chaotic right now, but I love you, and I want us to work toward being a family." He moved his hand to her stomach and was surprised to find it a little fuller than it had been. His eyes welled with tears. "I won't push you too hard. I just want to be here for you and for our baby."

Jason felt Gwen shaking slightly, and he realized she was crying.

"I want that, too," she said, almost in a whisper, her voice made soft by her sobs.

Jason wrapped his arms tightly around Gwen, stroking her hair and feeling the weight of the world lift from his chest.

* * *

Gwen left her apartment reluctantly. Jason was in the shower, and she was due to pick up her mother in twenty minutes. Having finally had a breakthrough with Jason, Gwen was not at all excited about having to spend the afternoon with her mother.

True, Leann had been unusually well behaved during her visit. She'd listened with interest as Gwen discussed her work and her projects for the city. She'd helped with the last-minute preparations for Val's wedding, and even offered to house-sit for Val and John while they were off on their honeymoon, an offer they politely declined, to Gwen's immense relief.

Was it possible that Leann had finally decided to be a mother? Taking a moment to stroke her own belly, which was noticeably rounder, at least to her, a little part of Gwen hoped so. But it was hard to ignore thirty years of neglect and abandonment. Gwen was suspicious of Leann's intentions, despite her good behavior.

Pulling up at the hotel entrance, Gwen was irritated to find Leann nowhere in sight. They agreed to meet outside so Gwen wouldn't have to park, but Leann had never been terribly concerned with inconveniencing other people. The little spark of hope in Gwen's mind evaporated. She growled and parked her car.

Gwen walked into the lobby and sank into a plush armchair. She pulled out her phone and called her mother.

"Hello?" Leann's voice sounded surprised.

"Hello to you. I'm in the lobby. You're supposed to be down here."

"Is it time already? I'm sorry, Gwen. Alex and I have been sitting here chatting, and I completely lost track of time."

"Well, I'm hungry so I'm leaving in five minutes. Be down here or I'm leaving without you." Gwen disconnected before Leann said anything further. It irked her to no end that Leann and Alex had taken such a liking to each other. On the one hand, it kept Leann distracted and away from Gwen for much of the week. On the other hand, Gwen couldn't help but worry about her mother's motives in befriending Alex. Leann rarely did anything that did not have a direct benefit for Leann.

Five minutes later, Gwen was standing to leave when her mother came strolling across the lobby.

"My, my, aren't we cranky today?" Leann said with a smile.

"Just hungry, Mom. I talked to you twenty minutes ago, and you said you'd meet me at the door."

"Forgive me for taking an interest in that poor lonely girl." Leann nodded toward the elevator. Gwen almost expected to see Alex walking toward them, but, thankfully, the lobby was empty. Without another word, Gwen turned and walked toward her car with her mother on her heels.

They drove to the restaurant in silence. It wasn't until they'd found a table at the restaurant and ordered drinks that either dared speak. Once again, Leann brought up Alex.

"It's nice Jason has taken such an interest in Alex." Gwen stiffened but tried to keep her reactions in check. She knew Leann was goading her. "I'm sure they keep each other from getting too lonely when they're out of town."

"What are your plans?" Gwen asked, curtly, desperate to change the subject.

"What do you mean, darling?" Leann asked, innocently. "I'm having lunch with you."

"What I mean is, how much longer are you going to stay?"

Leann assumed an expression of profound hurt that didn't quite reach her eyes. "Are you ready to get rid of me so quickly?" When Gwen didn't jump in to offer solace, Leann continued. "I told Jack you wouldn't be happy to see me."

Gwen stiffened. "When did you talk to Dad?"

"Last night. He wanted to come with me, but I assured him you'd be less than happy to see him."

"Come with you?"

"Oh, didn't I tell you? Your father and I got back together. About two years ago. We're married again!" Leann smiled, clearly expecting Gwen to be excited by the news.

"What are you talking about?" Gwen's heart began to race. It had been years since she'd even heard from her father. The idea that her parents had gotten back together and even remarried without bothering to mention it was repugnant.

With a dreamy look in her eyes, Leann said, "Oh, we've dated off and on for years. Since you were little. But a few years ago, we decided to move in together, and it was like going back in time. Back to the good old days."

"You mean the days before you had me?" Gwen said coldly.

"Don't be sulky, Gwen. It's not as if you've ever taken an interest in our lives."

Anger swelled in Gwen. "An interest in *your* lives? Are you kidding me?" Her shoulders tensed, and she folded her hands in her lap, trying to keep calm but failing miserably. "Why should I take an interest in your lives, Mother? You've both spent every day of my entire life making sure I knew how little you care about me, how you wished you'd never had me."

"Oh, Gwen. You're being so dramatic," Leann said, but she looked uncomfortable. Leann loved to stir things up, but she never stayed around long enough to deal with the repercussions.

"Why are you here, Mother? To see Val get married? Why? You aren't even close." Gwen voice shook.

"She's marrying into the Hatfields! How could I miss it?"

"John Hatfield and his family are some of the best people I know. How dare you treat Val's marriage as a spectacle!" Gwen's voice grew louder. People at neighboring tables were starting to look in their direction.

"Keep your voice down, Gwen. You're the mayor, aren't you? You can't go around half-cocked."

"You're certainly one to talk about making a scene," Gwen hissed. Her anger formed a knot in her stomach, but she regained control over her voice.

Ever the drama queen, Leann fanned herself. "You have no idea how hard it is, being a mother. You try to do right by your children, and all they do is abuse you."

"Oh, please. When have you ever been a mother to me?" Gwen's voice took on a dangerous tone. "My aunt was more a mother to me than you ever were. I remember you telling your friends that I was your *accident*. And you laughed, Mom. Do you know how that made me feel?" Gwen felt tears forming, but she was hell bent on keeping them at bay.

"Of course I told them that. You *were* an accident, Gwen. It's not mean. It's the truth. You know your father and I never meant to have children."

"Of course I know that. You've told me a million times. But you know what, Mom? Accident or no, the minute you decided to keep me, you owed me a better life than the one you gave me. I deserved love and compassion. You're right about one thing, you weren't meant to be a mother." The force of Gwen's words shocked her.

"Wait until you have kids, Gwen. You'll see how hard it is." Her mother's eyes were defiant, but her voice wavered.

Gwen gently placed her napkin on the table. "When I have kids, I will make sure they feel loved, every single day of their lives." Gwen stood, pulling on her coat and grabbing her purse. Before walking away from Leann, she said, "You can get a cab back to the hotel. Have a good trip home, Mom. I wish you and Dad every happiness. Don't worry about keeping in touch."

* * *

When she reached her car, Gwen slumped into the driver's seat and cried. For the longest time, she let the tears roll down her cheeks unchecked, forming puddles in her lap. She thought about that little girl who'd made her own costume back in grade school. She thought about the baby in her belly and the grandmother who'd never care. Lost in her grief, Gwen was startled to hear a knock at her window. She looked up and was surprised to find Evan McDaniel staring at her.

"Gwen," he said loudly, "Are you okay?"

Gwen rolled down the window an inch and said, "Evan. What are you doing here?"

Evan's eyes went to his feet. He shifted uncomfortably. "I … uh …"

"Why are you following me?" Gwen's voice was heavy with exhaustion. She wiped away her tears.

Evan's shoulder slumped. "I don't know." He shifted from one foot to the other. "I guess I thought maybe you'd change your mind about going out with me."

Gwen sighed, "Evan, you can't follow me around. I went to the police the other day because you're starting to scare me."

Evan's face drained of color. "The police?" He gulped. "Oh, no, I'm so sorry. I've been so stupid."

"You're not stupid, Evan. But surely you guessed this wasn't okay?" His expression confirmed it. "You have to stop this. Following me and sending flowers. It's all too over the top. You're going to get yourself in trouble, and I promise it's not going to end up the way you want it to."

Evan looked even more shaken. "Flowers? What are you talking about?"

Gwen hesitated, feeling even more uneasy. "I've been getting flowers at home and at work. I assumed they were from you since you've been following me."

"N … no, of course not," Evan stuttered. He looked terrified. "I never sent you flowers. Just the ones I brought you that day in your office. But those were from the whole committee."

Gwen felt sorry for the poor kid, but she was equally irritated the flowers were still a mystery. The weight of the day wore on Gwen. She needed to get home.

"Look, Evan. I've got to go. Please promise me you will stay away." Gwen's words felt very cruel, but she continued, determined to put this issue to rest. "When I said no, I meant it. If you keep following me, I will call the police. I believe you when you say you're sorry, so please don't make me regret not pressing this further."

Shame distorted Evan's features. He nodded silently, and walked quickly away from Gwen's car, his head tucked into his chest.

For a few moments, Gwen felt horrible about being so stern with Evan. She remembered her college years and how awkward she'd always felt around the opposite sex. Then again, it would never have occurred to her to actually stalk someone who'd rejected her. She sat back in her seat, contemplating kids today and then realized how old she sounded. Pulling out of the parking lot, she took one last look at the restaurant. She saw her mother, still sitting at the table they'd shared. Instead of sadness, Gwen felt closure.

CHAPTER TWENTY-SIX

Jason boarded the plane for California with a smile on his face. He felt lighter than he had in months. Despite the showdown between Gwen and her mother, he and Gwen ended the weekend on a good note. Jason would give notice to his landlord and move into Gwen's apartment in a few weeks. Gwen seemed genuinely happy about this turn of events, and Jason could hardly believe their relationship had taken such a positive turn.

The first few days of the week went by smoothly. Alex stayed with her family, which gave Jason some much-needed breathing space. When he saw her in the office, he kept things professional. Friendly, but not overly interested. It wasn't difficult. His infatuation with Alex seemed to have disappeared. Whether it was due to having made up with Gwen, or his lingering irritation with Alex for having chummed up with Gwen's mom. It didn't matter. Jason felt back to normal.

Then, late Wednesday evening, Alex approached him about having dinner the following night.

"There's this great place down on the boardwalk. I haven't been there in years, but my aunt says they have a new cook, and the food is to die for."

Jason hesitated. "I'm not sure. My flight leaves right after work on Friday, so I want to get packed."

Alex crinkled her nose. "Come on. We'll only be out for a while. I haven't seen much of you this week. It'll be fun!"

That perkiness had drawn Jason to Alex in the first place. It reminded him of Gwen, the way she was before being the mayor took all the fun out of life. Once again, Jason wondered if he'd been imagining her interest based on his own conflicted feelings. Alex was a friendly person. Maybe he was reading too much into her actions. Finally, he relented.

"Okay, but I want to get back early."

Alex beamed. "Great! I'll meet you here after work tomorrow." She walked away with a bounce in her step.

Jason got back to work, quickly immersing himself in the problem at hand. The California office was having issues. One department was continually under-producing, and there seemed to be some staffing issues. Jason's job was to analyze the situation and report back to his division head, making recommendations about cutbacks to ease the financial burden the department posed to the corporation.

Jason had been over this particular set of records twice now, and he suspected that what appeared on its surface to be mismanagement of funds might actually be something worse. There was one employee in the department whose expense tracking lacked the requisite documentation, and Jason was almost ready to present his findings to his boss. Being new, he wanted to triple check his work, knowing the findings could be used against this employee.

By close of business, he was satisfied with his report. He called his boss's secretary and scheduled a Skype call for ten o'clock the following morning.

Back at his hotel, Jason pulled out his trusty peanut butter, grabbed a spoon and lay back on his bed to watch the news. Several scoops in, he chuckled. *This is probably not the most healthy way to eat peanut butter,* he mused. Having gotten her appetite back in a big way, he caught Gwen regularly eating peanut butter out of the container at home. The thought made him smile.

As if on cue, his phone started buzzing.

"Hey, honey. I was thinking about you."

"Oh?" Gwen sounded sleepy.

"Eating peanut butter out of the jar."

Gwen giggled. "That's my move."

"I know," Jason said, smiling. "I think it's cuter when you do it. Something decidedly sad about a grown man sitting on a hotel bed with a jar of peanut butter."

"Hey, what works, works. So you didn't go out?" Jason thought he detected a hint of uneasiness in Gwen's voice.

"No. But Alex asked me to join her for dinner tomorrow night." Jason heard Gwen's sigh loud and clear. "I understand your reservations about Alex."

"I really don't mean to be jealous, Jason. In fact, it feels terrible. But there's something about her that makes me nervous. I felt like our whole lunch the other day was a contest. Or at least, I think she wanted to make sure I knew you two were close. I think she likes you quite a lot."

Jason cringed. Maybe he wasn't imagining Alex's interest in him. "If it makes you this uncomfortable, I'll cancel."

It took a moment for Gwen to respond, but she finally said, "No. I really don't want you to cancel. I know traveling must be lonely, and I don't want to stop you from having friendships. I'm really jumpy right now." Jason pictured Gwen rubbing her belly, a new frequent habit. He grinned.

"I love you, Gwen. I'm not going anywhere, and when I get home Friday, we'll start working on our next steps."

"Deal. I'm going to go eat some horribly salty food because it sounds good and then sleep for ten hours." Gwen laughed. "I could get used to this pregnancy stuff."

"Good, because I think we should have ten kids," Jason said, smiling.

"Good luck with that plan, super stud. What do you say we work on baby number one and see how it goes?"

They said their goodbyes and disconnected. Jason put aside the peanut butter jar and lay back, staring at the ceiling and contemplating his new life. He and Gwen would be having a baby next summer. She'd finally agreed to living with him. The only catch now was Jason's job. When he'd taken the BGB job, he'd been so frustrated with life in Cambria that being absent seemed like a good way to ease his growing tension. Now he realized how much he was going to miss. Given how independent Gwen was, he knew she could deal with his absences, but how would he feel when he became a father?

He thought about Gwen and her family. Jason always thought of Gwen as an incredibly balanced person, but having her mother in town had been an eye-opener. A mostly absent father and a neglectful mother left Gwen with some insecurities she worked very hard to mask. Jason didn't want his child growing up feeling unloved. He knew Gwen would make a wonderful mother, but he was just as sure he wanted to be a wonderful father, one who was present in his children's lives.

He spent the rest of the evening thinking about his life, his family and his options for getting his work schedule into alignment with his personal priorities.

* * *

The next day, Alex popped up at Jason's desk right at five o'clock.

"Ready? I'm starving!"

Jason smiled. His meeting with the boss had gone really well, and Jason felt accomplished. "Yes. Let me save this file, and I'll be ready to go."

Shutting down his computer, Jason grabbed his jacket and followed Alex out to the parking garage.

"I borrowed my uncle's car for tonight," she said, pointing at a blue Toyota sedan a few spots from the front gate. "It's a little bit of a drive to the restaurant."

They headed out onto the highway. Jason looked out at the

ocean, the sun dipping below the horizon. They were heading out of town.

"Where is this restaurant?" he asked, raising an eyebrow.

Alex smiled. "It's a few miles out of town."

"I thought it was on the boardwalk?" Jason began to feel uncomfortable.

"It's on the beach, and there's a beautiful pier nearby, so that counts right?"

Jason felt flush with irritation, but he remained quiet, peering out the window at the surf below.

"Have you been out this way?" Alex asked, casually.

"No, I've been sticking pretty close to the hotel and the office."

"I used to love visiting this area when I was a kid. The restaurant we're going to is in the lobby of this great little boutique hotel. My brother and I used to dare each to jump off the pier but it's really high, and I was always too chicken."

Jason smiled at the image. "Hard to imagine. You seem pretty fearless." He was still annoyed, but decided to give Alex the benefit of the doubt and relax. Talk about her childhood seemed innocent enough.

Alex kept her eyes on the winding road. "I'm a good actress. I'm scared of all kinds of things."

"Like what?" Jason asked, genuinely curious.

"Let's see. I'm terrified of spiders, even the ones I know are good. Like tarantulas. Bleh. We have them out in the desert, and I can't stand the sight of them."

"Okay, spiders. That's not so unusual. What else?"

Alex glanced over, giving him a very meaningful look before turning her eyes back to the road. "I'm afraid of being alone. Of never falling in love again. Or ... of not being loved in return."

Jason was quiet for a moment. "That won't happen, Alex. You're a great person."

Alex beamed. "Oh, look." She pointed out the window. "There it is!"

Off to the right, a piece of land jutted out into the water. There was a large house with a wraparound porch facing the ocean. Jason saw the lights of the pier stretching out over the water.

"That's a hotel?" Jason asked skeptically. The house looked much too small to hold a restaurant and a hotel.

"It's small. It's more like a bed and breakfast, I think. Only a few guest rooms. The restaurant is very cozy."

This was an understatement. On entering the front door, Jason saw the so-called restaurant was really a tiny dining area consisting of only three small tables. A fire roared in the fireplace by the back wall. There was nobody around. Just as Jason starting feeling nervous, a gray-haired woman in a floral print farm dress came out from the kitchen area.

"Oh! You're here. I'm sorry, I didn't hear you pull up. You're our only guests tonight so I'm helping in the kitchen. I'm Emma. Welcome to the Huckleberry Inn." She reached out a hand to Jason and Alex. "Your room is ready, as is your table. If you'd like to leave your bags in the lobby, my husband Hank will take them up."

Jason looked at Alex, confused. "Our room?"

"They only serve dinner for guests, so I booked a room."

Emma raised an eyebrow. "You're not staying?" The look on Emma's face oozed disapproval, and Jason could tell she was biting her tongue, which made him blush.

"No, we're just here for dinner," Jason said, feeling tense.

Emma looked from Alex to Jason and then said, hesitantly. "Let's get you seated and fed." She led them to their table, a two-top near the fireplace. There were fresh flowers and a candle flickering in a gilded holder.

"What's going on, Alex?" Jason asked, his voice tight, his expression stern.

Alex shrugged, averting her eyes from his penetrating stare. "I've always wanted to come back here, and I wasn't aware of the guest-only policy. When I called to make reservations, I decided to go for it. The room was inexpensive." Alex looked around the room, letting her eyes settle everywhere but on Jason.

"I don't feel comfortable about this," Jason started, but at that moment, Emma appeared with a bottle of wine.

"The grapes for this wine are grown right down the road." She poured two glasses, and, sensing the tension between Alex and Jason, she asked, "Is something wrong, loves?"

Not wanting to be rude, Jason looked at her and said, kindly. "No, ma'am." He picked up his menu. "Everything looks delicious. What do you recommend?"

Relieved, Emma said, "French onion soup is our specialty. And the salmon is very fresh, so I'd recommend one of those. Or both, if you're hungry. And our chocolate cake is divine." She winked. "I made it myself."

Jason smiled. "Okay, I'll have the French onion soup, the salmon, and a big heaping slice of the chocolate cake."

Alex looked relieved. "Me too."

Emma took their menus and walked back to the kitchen. Determined to get through the evening without more conflict, Jason launched into a discussion about their current project at work, hoping the topic would keep things between them nice and boring long enough to get through this awkward night.

Alex's normally shiny disposition seemed to have lost some of its luster, but she did her best to keep up in the conversation. After three glasses of wine, Alex's cheeks glowed, and Jason felt certain she'd had too much to drink. He scraped the last of his chocolate cake off his plate. It certainly was divine.

"Are you ready to head back?" Jason asked, though he could see she was not.

Alex looked at him, her face full of anguish as she said, "Would it be okay if we take a walk on the pier? I think I need to sober up."

Jason sighed. "Okay. But I should probably drive back."

Alex nodded and walked toward the door, stumbling a bit.

They reached the pier and walked silently toward the water. "I'm sorry, Jason. I don't usually drink this much." "I thought that might be the case. Only three glasses. You're a lightweight." Jason tried to keep the conversation casual, but there was something very desperate in Alex's tone.

About halfway down the pier, she stopped and turned to Jason. "I need to be honest with you, Jason. I like you. A lot. I think about you all the time." She hesitated. "We have fun together. I haven't felt this way about anyone since my husband and I split up."

Jason wanted to interrupt her, to save her from the humiliation she was sure to feel when she sobered up. But she put up a hand, stopping him from saying a word.

"Just hear me out, okay? I've been watching you over the past few months, and I can see what you and Gwen have isn't working. You're miserable with her, Jason. And you're happy with me." Her eyes were pleading. "Can't you consider for a moment that I'm the one you should be with?"

Alex's expression was so hopeful Jason couldn't bring himself to express the anger he felt at being set up. Instead, he said, "I can't, Alex." Unsure how to proceed, he looked down, studying his shoes. When he lifted his gaze to Alex, she was crying. In spite of himself, Jason felt incredibly guilty.

Awkwardly, he wrapped an arm around her shoulder. "Don't cry, Alex. I meant what I said. You're a great person, and you'll find someone who's right for you." Alex's arms wrapped around his waist, and he stiffened. Her face turned up, and she pressed her lips into his, kissing him passionately.

For a moment, Jason was too shocked to respond. Then he pulled his head away and pushed Alex's arms from his body. Alex's arms hung at her side limply. Tears spilled down her cheeks as she sobbed, dejected.

Without a word, Jason turned and walked to the car, leaving Alex standing on the pier, a lone figure against the expanse of the moonlit ocean. Jason leaned against Alex's car, lost in thought. When she finally approached, she handed him the keys and walked silently to the passenger side. They drove back in silence. When Jason pulled into the hotel driveway, he turned to Alex. "I'm sorry, Alex. Under the circumstances, I think we shouldn't see each other outside the office anymore."

She nodded, but stayed silent. Jason got out of the car, leaving the keys in the ignition so that Alex could reclaim the driver's seat. She slipped by him sulkily, sank behind the wheel, and pulled away from the curb.

CHAPTER TWENTY-SEVEN

After their disastrous evening together, Alex called in sick on Friday. Jason was being called back to Denver to help sort out the issue with the errant department he'd audited. Not having to deal with her for a whole week gave Jason the room he needed to figure out how to move forward without the added distraction. After work every day in Denver, he packed boxes and moved things into Gwen's apartment.

Gwen was getting ready to go to a Mayor's Conference in Denver over the weekend. She spent several hours each night working on her presentation about women in politics, practicing different parts with Jason, and then incorporating his feedback. Her determination reminded him of the old Gwen, the one who became mayor against all odds. It was nice to see things come full circle.

Thursday evening, Gwen met Jason in Denver for dinner.

"I decided to stay with Victoria during the conference. It'll be nice to catch up." Gwen moved her potatoes across her plate.

"Are you feeling okay?" Jason said, noticing her restlessness.

"I'm nervous about my talk tomorrow." Gwen crinkled her nose. "And these potatoes don't taste right to me."

Jason leaned over and plucked a spud off her plate, popping it in his mouth. "Tastes pretty good to me."

Gwen sighed. "I thought that might be the case. Some things don't work for me right now." She shifted in her seat. "And I'm starting to feel like I have a perpetually full stomach, even when I'm starving. It's strange." Her hand wandered to her belly. "I need to announce my pregnancy at work."

Jason nodded. Gwen's belly had become visibly rounder, and he knew it wasn't long before other people started to notice. "Is Karen still backing off?"

"Yes, but I can tell she's seething, which makes me nervous. I've resigned myself to the idea that work is going to be unpleasant." Gwen's face drooped. "I never imagined being the mayor would be this depressing."

Jason took her hand. "Hang in there. I got you something." Jason reached into his coat pocket and handed Gwen a small box wrapped in silver ribbon.

The look of sheer panic on Gwen's face made Jason laugh out loud. "Don't worry, it's just a little something."

Gwen opened the box and gasped. Resting on a little satin pillow was a silver bracelet with three small loops. It was simple and delicate. When Gwen looked up at Jason, there were tears in her eyes.

"What's this for?" she said, her voice trembling.

"It's for good luck," he said, smiling. "And to remind you of all the wonderful things life has in store for us."

Gwen ran her finger over the little loops. "Will you help me put it on?"

Jason came around to her side of the table, lifting the delicate metal and placing it gently around Gwen's wrist. As he fastened it, he said, "You, me, and baby." Gwen reached up and put her arms around Jason's neck.

"Thank you. It's perfect," she said, and then kissed him.

Jason went back to his chair. "You'll be home Sunday?"

Gwen nodded. "Not until around four. I'm going to have lunch with Vic after the conference ends."

"My plan is to get the rest of my stuff moved this weekend and then hopefully start cleaning my apartment."

Gwen grinned. "Perfect timing. For me." She winked at him. "Yes, I realize you're heartbroken." He laughed. "It looks like I'll be back in California next week. I have a few things to resolve with the team, and then I'm back in Arizona."

Gwen became distracted. "Jason," she started, but paused as if trying to find the courage to say more. "I need to tell you something."

Looking concerned, Jason put down his fork and waited.

"About Alex." Jason felt his heart race, but he kept his expression neutral.

"Oh?"

"When I had lunch with Mom, she made comments that made me think Alex was talking to her about you, implying that she's interested in you." Again, Gwen paused. Jason felt his face flush.

"Like what?" he asked, worried about what Alex might have confessed to Leann. He'd decided not to mention Alex's ill-fated attempt to win him over, and was worried she'd think he'd kept it from her.

Gwen sighed. "Honestly, I don't trust a thing Leann says, since it's clear she's always trying to stir things up. And I don't really want to spend any more time thinking about my mother or her gossip-mongering. But it left me feeling vulnerable."

Jason cringed. "What a mess. It's too bad Alex and Leann crossed paths. But you don't have anything to worry about."

Gwen nodded and continued. "I wasn't sure whether I should even tell you." Then she frowned. "But I think Leann is probably right."

Jason sighed. "She is." Gwen's shoulders stiffened. "The other night when Alex asked me out to dinner, she confessed her feelings. I told her I wasn't interested and suggested we shouldn't hang out anymore given how she felt." Jason hoped he wouldn't have to go into details. He still felt guilty about the kiss, even though he hadn't returned it, and about how crushed Alex looked when she'd pulled away from the curb.

Gwen nodded.

"I get the feeling Alex hasn't gotten over her divorce. But I've made it very clear where I stand."

Gwen reached for Jason's hand and gave it a squeeze. "I love you."

"I love you, too."

Gwen sighed. "I'm going to go over my presentation again. I'm really worried about my job right now, and, if this is the last thing I do as mayor, I want to make an impact."

"It's going to be okay, Gwen. They can't fire you because you're pregnant."

"I know," she said, but she was plagued by doubt.

CHAPTER TWENTY-EIGHT

Gwen entered the lobby of the Four Seasons hotel and headed toward the conference registration desk. She'd put aside her sensible black suit in favor of her trendier wool suit with knee high boots and a colorful scarf. She had a moment of panic at Victoria's apartment when she could barely zip up the skirt. It wouldn't be long before the world took notice of her expanding form.

"Gwen?" The voice came from behind her. She turned around and was face to face with Constance Carlton, the First Lady of Colorado.

"Hi Constance." Gwen gave her a hug. "I didn't realize I'd see you here."

"I don't usually attend, but this year, my favorite mayor is giving a presentation on women in politics, so I popped over."

"No pressure there," Gwen laughed, though her nerves were a little jumbled.

"Don't worry, Gwen," Constance said, smiling. "I'll behave myself in the back of the room. I wanted to hear your talk and … the Governor asked me to remind you about his offer."

"Oh, my goodness, I cannot believe this! I totally forgot. So much has happened since we talked about it, I didn't even have his offer on my radar."

Constance raised an eyebrow. "Anything good?"

Gwen blushed. "One thing. But you can't tell a soul, okay? I'm pregnant."

Constance's hand went to her mouth to stop a squeal, but she smiled. Making sure to keep her voice low, she said, "Congratulations, Gwen! That's exciting news. You look fantastic, by the way. When are you due?"

"June second. I've got a long way to go, but these clothes are starting to get a little uncomfortable."

Constance giggled. "I know exactly how you feel. I started sewing panels into my dress pants and skirts by ten weeks." She chuckled. "Of course, I wouldn't recommend gaining nearly as much weight as I did with my firstborn."

"You know, it's funny. I've been terrified about how everyone at work is going to react to this pregnancy. I keep forgetting other woman have managed to have babies and still work."

Constance patted Gwen on the arm. "It's an adjustment, certainly, but nothing you can't handle." Glancing past Gwen, Constance said, "Sorry Gwen, I have to go snag someone before they get away. The Governor's orders." She kissed Gwen on the cheek and hurried past toward a group of women across the lobby.

Gwen made her way toward the conference room. She had a few hours before she was scheduled to present, and there was a session on youth engagement starting soon that Gwen wanted to attend. She made her way down the hall, and found a seat at the edge of the room near the door in case she needed to make a quick escape. She'd had several cups of tea, and if she'd learned one thing about being pregnant, it was that her bladder was not her ally.

Gwen listened with rapt attention as the presenter outlined practical ways to get young people involved in local politics and how to increase voter turnout. Her notebook was so covered in notes that she hoped she could read later. Before she knew it, it was time to go and prepare for her own presentation.

Finding her assigned room, Gwen walked to the front of the empty space, put her bag down and took a deep breath.

"Gwen Marsh?" A young woman approached from the back of the room. She wore a conference staff t-shirt, her long sleek black hair hung down to her waist. "I'm Angie, your room monitor. Do you have your presentation ready to plug in?"

"Yes." Gwen she pulled the laptop out of her bag, handing it to Angie.

As Angie plugged the computer into the projector, she smiled at Gwen. "I'm a huge fan of yours, Ms. Marsh. I'm a student here in Denver, and I followed your campaign last year. I want to go into politics too, so it's great to see another young woman able to make a stand."

Gwen's cheeks grew hotter. This girl was probably more than a decade her junior, but she talked about Gwen as if they were contemporaries. It made Gwen's chest swell with pride at the work she'd done and the pathway she'd paved in her own way.

"Thank you, Angie. That means a lot to me. Please, call me Gwen." She held out her to hand to Angie. "If you ever want to come spend the day with me, I'd be happy to show you around City Hall and give you an insider's view of my job."

Angie beamed. "That would be so amazing!" The girl's enthusiasm was palpable. "My parents live in Cambria so I go stay with them some weekends. We all voted for you."

Gwen's presentation popped up on the screen.

"Okay, Gwen. Here's your clicker." Angie handed her a remote to use during her talk. "It's RF so you don't have to point it at the projector, just click. I'm going to be sitting at that front table, so I'll hold up a sign when you have ten minutes, then five, then two, then time. Is that okay?"

Gwen couldn't help but smile. Angie reminded her of herself when she was in college, ready to take on the world and prove herself. *It's funny how easily the world can beat you down if you let it*, Gwen thought. "Perfect. Thanks Angie, you've been a huge help."

Angie retired to her seat as people started coming into the

room. Gwen saw Constance near the back, with a group of women Gwen thought she recognized but couldn't place. Her mind began to wander, so she picked up her notes and studied them, hoping to stay focused. When the room settled, Gwen began to speak.

"'Do what you feel in your heart to be right—for you'll be criticized anyway. You'll be damned if you do and damned if you don't.' Anyone know who said that?" Gwen scanned the room, but no one volunteered. She didn't expect them to, at least not yet.

"Eleanor Roosevelt was our longest seated First Lady of the United States. Her work and influence were felt during the years her husband was in office, and long after. Eleanor was criticized for her outspokenness. She advocated for women to become true citizens by becoming involved in politics, by voting and running for office. She knew the obstacles women would face in these new roles, having faced those obstacles herself."

The audience listened with rapt attention. All side conversations stopped. Gwen felt herself relax.

"What about this one? 'It is past time for women to take their rightful place, side by side with men, in the rooms where the fates of peoples, where their children's and grandchildren's fates, are decided.'"

This time a few hands went up. Gwen chose one woman at random.

"Hillary Clinton?" the woman said, shyly.

Gwen smiled. "Don't be afraid to speak up. Yes, Hillary Clinton, our Democratic nominee for the Presidency. The first woman ever to achieve the nomination for this job. Almost seventy years after Eleanor Roosevelt was criticized not only her outspokenness but also for her appearance. In running for President of the United States, Hillary Clinton has been criticized for everything from official actions to her clothing choices and hairstyle. So I ask you, have we made progress? Have we attained Clinton's ideal of equality for men and women in the rooms where fates are decided?"

A collective murmur of *no* echoed through the room, and Gwen saw most of the attendees shaking their heads.

"Last year, I was elected as mayor of the city of Cambria. I was criticized for my inexperience and my youth, but also for my appearance. Someone told me I was too pretty to be in politics." Gwen paused. "I can't think of anything more insulting to say to someone who has devoted her life to politics. But women who choose to enter the political arena bear the history of all the women who have come before them."

For the next hour, Gwen talked about some of her favorite political figures, both women and men, who'd stood against seemingly insurmountable opposition to fight for the right of women to vote and to participate in every level of politics. As she spoke, the crowd responded, nodding approval and applauding. Gwen's spirit soared as she worked the crowd, taking questions and relating anecdotes from her own time in office. Before she knew it, Angie held up the two-minute warning sign.

Smiling, Gwen said. "It looks like my time is up. But I want to thank all of you, my fellow mayors and politicians, for continuing to forge a path for all people to participate actively and passionately in making those decisions that chart the course for our futures. It's been an honor to talk with you today, and I hope you'll stay in touch."

The audience applauded boisterously, with several people rising to their feet. Gwen smiled warmly, proud of the speech but also happy to feel that connection with the crowd. In the past few months, her work as mayor had been so full of stress and subterfuge she'd almost forgotten the real reason she'd run for mayor; to make an impact. It felt good to let her passion flow, to talk about things that stirred emotions within her and, possibly, to send these people away with a renewed sense of purpose.

* * *

The crowd began to exit, heading toward their next sessions, but a few stragglers came forward to shake Gwen's hand and congratulate her on her election victory. At the end of the queue was a tall, slender woman with long brown hair tied back in a ponytail. She approached Gwen.

"That was a wonderful presentation," she said, smiling. "I'm Christine Berg. I'm the mayor of Lafayette."

Gwen shook Christine's hand. "I've read a lot about your work on clean air initiatives."

"Thank you." Christine smiled. "I've been really focused on health and lifestyle in my community. It's nice to live so close to Boulder. It's a very health-conscious community so there's a lot of support. Now, my low-income housing initiatives are trickier."

"I empathize in a big way." Gwen chuckled. "Cambria has a very small but vocal contingent who seem to go out of their way to fight those types of programs, especially when property taxes are part of the conversation."

"I definitely know the feeling." Christine's phone buzzed, and she spent a moment reading the text she'd received. She laughed. "My husband took my daughter to the children's museum, and, apparently she was so wiped out, she fell asleep in the car. He'll be suffering later. Morning naps mean cranky princesses in the afternoon."

Mayor Berg's easy manner as she talked about her family gave Gwen an idea.

"Can I ask you something?"

"Of course."

Gwen hesitated before asking, "How do you do it? How do you manage to be a mother and the mayor?"

Christine chuckled. "Ah, the million-dollar question." Tossing her phone back in her bag, she continued, "It's a juggling act. And it's not always easy. In fact, I'd say it's rarely easy, but it is so worth it." She smiled. "Want to go grab some coffee and talk about it?"

"Yes, please. That would be wonderful."

They made their way to the hotel coffee shop, stopping to shake hands with colleagues as they went. Gwen ordered a cup of tea while Christine settled in with a large steaming mocha. Gwen inhaled deeply, savoring the forbidden aroma of the caffeinated beverage.

"Do you have children?" Christine asked between sips.

"No," Gwen said, then paused. "But I'm pregnant. I wasn't expecting to have to deal with having a family while in office, at least not so soon. I'm not married, and I'm not sure I'm ready to deal with people's negativity."

Christine smiled. "I can understand that. I was pregnant with my daughter while I was a councilwoman. Most people were kind and encouraging. The other council members even threw me a baby shower." She chuckled. "But there were also those people who felt it was their responsibility to let me know how many ways I was failing my family by being a working mother."

"How did you deal with that?"

"I ignored them. Sometimes I cried. The funny thing is that while I don't consider myself a failure by any means, it is true my work as mayor has taken a toll on my family. It's a part-time job, but I work full-time hours. There are evening events and travel." Christine paused. "I've been incredibly lucky because my husband's schedule is flexible, and I work from home. I'm not sure it would work otherwise, and there are times when I think my husband is tired of the strain."

Gwen was encouraged by the honesty in Christine's words. Everybody kept telling her how they knew she could do it, but it was relieving to hear someone talk about the reality of being a mother and a public servant.

"How old is your daughter?"

"She's five." Christine pulled out her phone and showed

Gwen a photo. "She's the best thing that ever happened for me. I take her with me to my office sometimes and the city staff has become really fond of her."

Gwen smiled. "She's adorable. What does she think of you being the mayor?"

Christine laughed. "She's only five so she doesn't really understand what I do. But she loves when I take her to council chambers and let her sit in my chair. And we get to go to all the fun city events. She loves that too."

Gwen sighed. "You have no idea how much it means to me, talking to you like this. I've felt so alone in this."

Christine reached out and took Gwen's hand. "I think we all feel that way sometimes, but like you said in your presentation, we bear the history of the women who've come before us." She winked. "And we pave the way for the women who will follow in our footsteps."

CHAPTER TWENTY-NINE

When Gwen walked into her apartment on Sunday afternoon, she was met by savory smells and a beaming Jason, who had prepared a candlelight dinner. He'd been busy cleaning and organizing the apartment.

"Hey, beautiful," he said, taking her bag and wrapping his arms around her. "How'd the conference go?"

Gwen smiled, taking in the feel of his arms and the smell of his clothes. "It was really, really great, actually. My talk went well, and I met the mayor of Lafayette. Did you know she was pregnant in office? She was on the city council at the time, but she managed to have her daughter and go on to run for mayor."

"That's awesome. Did you tell her?" He moved his hand gently along Gwen's belly.

"I did. She had some really great advice. I think I'm ready to tell everyone."

Jason kissed her forehead. "That's good. But first, I have a surprise for you."

"Oh?" Gwen said, her eyebrows rose suspiciously.

"Close your eyes and follow me."

Gwen closed her eyes and allowed herself to be led down the hall. She expected Jason to head to her bedroom, their bedroom now. That thought was a little shocking. Instead, he turned toward the small bedroom Gwen used as an office and storage room.

"You can open your eyes."

Gwen was amazed to find the room completely empty.

"What happened in here?" She asked, wondering where her desk and files had been moved. "You decided you need your own room?" she teased.

Jason grinned. "No. But I thought we might use this room as the nursery." His eyes twinkled. "I cleared out all the stuff and rearranged things a bit. We can pick out furniture and decorations together."

Gwen felt tears in her eyes. She hadn't even gotten as far as thinking about where the baby would be sleeping. She'd been so wrapped up in all the drama going on around her that she'd barely allowed herself a moment to think about the practical parts of having a baby. Cribs and layettes were not on her radar.

"Gwen?" She realized she'd gone completely still and silent. Jason's face had gone from elated to a little bit panicked. "Are you okay, honey?"

Gwen snuggled into Jason's chest, leading him to wrap his arm around her shoulder. "I can't believe you did all this. It's wonderful." She felt Jason relax.

"Oh, good. I was worried you'd be mad at me for moving all your stuff. But I got carried away."

Gwen smiled up at him. "You *will* have to tell me where my office has moved to eventually, but what do you say we spend the rest of the evening practicing at being parents-to-be."

"What do you have in mind?" Jason asked, his voice a little breathless.

"Well," Gwen started with a mischievous glint in her eye. "I thought maybe we could go test out the new bedroom before I'm so big you won't fit in bed with me." She winked.

Jason cleared his throat. "Mayor Marsh, you make a very good argument." He took her hand and led her to the bedroom. As they lay down together, Gwen chuckled at the stacks of boxes discarded around the room. *Oh boy*, she thought, and then turned her attention to Jason and the start of her new life.

* * *

Early Tuesday morning, Gwen sat in her chair in city council chambers, watching as people filed in and took seats. She'd emailed key staff and the other councilmen on Monday asking for a quick meeting on Tuesday morning before the building opened to the public. She hoped by scheduling the meeting just before everyone had to get to work, that she would discourage too many stragglers.

At five minutes to eight, Gwen started the meeting. "Good morning, everyone. I really appreciate you coming in early this morning. I have a quick announcement, and then I'll rely on everyone who was able to make it to inform their departments as they see fit."

The crowd stirred, unsure of what was coming.

"I wanted to let you all know I'm pregnant." As expected, nervous chatter erupted throughout the room. Gwen cleared her throat. "I know I could have sent an email, but I've worked so closely with all of you that I wanted to share the news in person." More hushed conversations. "I'm due next June. In the meantime, barring any unforeseen health issues, I plan on conducting business as usual until a few weeks before my due date. If you have any questions or concerns, please don't hesitate to let me know. Now, it's time to open the doors. Everyone have a wonderful day."

Gwen watched as people filed out of the room. She wondered what kind of backlash there would be, but now the cat was out of the bag, she realized she wasn't nearly as fearful as she had been. Gwen picked up her papers and headed toward her office. In the hall, she saw Karen Fredrickson heading her direction.

Oh boy, here we go.

"Needed another challenge, eh?" Karen said, as she approached. Her tone was less hostile than usual, but she frowned.

Gwen sighed. She'd tried to prepare herself for the negative comments, but she'd hoped to avoid them a little longer than this. Her emotional reaction was to let out a snarky comment, but instead, Gwen opted for brutal honesty. "Actually Karen, I'm terrified."

To Gwen's surprise, Karen's face softened. "I don't get you, Gwen. You've got everything going for you. Why in the world would you decide to have a baby right now?"

Gwen laughed. "This isn't some fairytale, Karen. I didn't plan it." Karen frowned, and Gwen wished she'd have kept her mouth shut, but it was too late now. She braced for an admonishment.

"Don't expect us to fall all over ourselves making accommodations for you just because you got yourself knocked up." Karen's face was full of spite, and her words cut Gwen to the bone. This was exactly the response she'd been expecting.

For a moment, Gwen felt her confidence falter. She took a deep breath and reflected on her meeting with Mayor Berg and the words of Eleanor Roosevelt that she'd used in her presentation. *You'll be criticized anyway,* she thought, and then she smiled. Confidence restored, Gwen knew what she had to say to naysayers, and it started here.

"If I've learned one thing in my life, it's that we don't always have control over the things that happen to us." Gwen put her hand on her belly. "But I refuse to believe that women" she looked meaningfully at Karen, "should have to choose between motherhood and their careers. I respect your work, Karen, and I know that my being here has made you feel insecure. But my personal life is none of your business, so unless it affects my work, I will thank you to keep your opinions to yourself."

Karen's cheeks flushed, but she nodded. "I'll let the staff know." She turned and walked back to her office.

Gwen walked into her office and sighed heavily. *Why do women make it so hard on each other?* She didn't expect things to be easy between her and Karen, but she'd be damned if she'd spend another moment feeling any shame about her decisions.

CHAPTER THIRTY

Jason paced outside his boss's office, looking at his watch on each lap. Every few minutes, he made eye contact with the secretary. He could tell he made her nervous, but his own nerves made it impossible to stop pacing.

"He can see you now," she said, nodding toward Bill Mackey's office door. Jason felt sluggish. He walked so slowly toward the door that the secretary looked at him with concern. Finally, he opened the door and walked in.

"Jason. How are you?"

Jason stepped up to Bill's desk, shaking his hand before taking a seat.

"What can I do for you?" Bill sat with his hands clasped on his desk, reminding Jason of a television boss waiting to give his employee some bad news. The thought was not comforting.

"I have something I'd like to discuss with you." He paused. "My girlfriend Gwen is pregnant. I took this position before we found out and now that things are progressing, I'm not sure I want to do this much traveling."

Bill frowned, and Jason looked down at his hands in his lap like a schoolboy awaiting his punishment. He'd only been working for BGB for a few months, and quitting now felt like career suicide, but the idea of not being around for his new family was not an option.

"When is the baby due?" Bill asked.

"June second. Gwen's the mayor in Cambria, where we live, and she plans on working right up until the end if she can. I should have another six months or so before I need to be closer to home." Jason looked around the room, searching for something to bolster his confidence.

"So you're resigning then?" his boss asked, his face stern.

"Not right away. I can help you train my replacement. I don't want to leave you guys in the lurch."

"Have you enjoyed working with BGB?" Bill asked.

Jason paused. This line of questioning was unexpected. He wondered if Bill would try to talk him into staying on board. "Yes, I have. The travel has been rough, but it's been really interesting working with the different facilities. Never a dull moment," Jason said, thinking about Alex and some of the non-work-related stressors that he wouldn't mind leaving behind.

Bill remained silent for a few moments. Then, he said, "Alright, Jason, I'll need a few days to think about the best course of action." Bill sat back in his chair. "You're flying out to Arizona this morning, right?"

"Right."

Checking his calendar, Bill said, "Let's plan a meeting at the Arizona plant on Wednesday at two o'clock?"

"I didn't realize you were coming down."

"Neither did I," Bill said, his tone giving away nothing about what he thought.

Jason stood. "I'll see you then." He headed straight to the airport from the Denver office. He hadn't told Gwen yet about his plans to quit his job. Though he knew it was a calculated risk telling his boss his plans this early, he hoped they'd appreciate his consideration and keep him on for a few months, giving him a chance to look for other jobs and, of course, train a replacement.

When he arrived in Arizona, Jason was concerned to find Alex waiting for him at baggage claim.

"Hey, Jason," she said, glumly.

"What are you doing here?" he asked, hoping he didn't sound too rude.

"I wanted to apologize before we got started this week." Alex paused, fidgeting with the hem of her shirt and shifting her weight from foot to foot. "And I need to tell you something."

"What's that?" Jason asked, suspiciously.

"I wanted you to know I sent Gwen flowers. A lot of flowers." Alex looked miserable. "When we first met, you mentioned pink roses were her favorite. Then it seemed like things weren't working between you two, so I decided to nudge things along."

"You've got to be kidding. That was a pretty shit move," Jason said, having decided being blunt was the best policy when dealing with Alex.

"I know. I'm not proud of myself. I don't know what I was thinking. I've been so lonely since my marriage broke up, and you were so nice to me."

"I don't understand. You were such a good friend to me when things weren't going very well in my life," Jason said, attempting to be charitable despite his misgivings. After all, he'd still be working with Alex.

"No, I wasn't. I was attracted to you from day one, and I saw your relationship was in trouble. I took advantage. Hell, I taunted Gwen the whole time we were together that day in Cambria. I sent those flowers hoping to break you two up." Alex stared down at her shoes. "Anyway, I wanted to apologize. I can't change what I've done, but I hope we can still work together without having any problems. This job really means a lot to me, and I don't want to lose it."

Jason nodded, too shocked by Alex's brutal honesty to know what to say.

"Can I give you a ride to the office?" Alex said, hopefully.

"No." Jason wanted to give Alex the benefit of the doubt, but he was on high alert, realizing how close he'd come to losing Gwen, how close Alex had come to succeeding in her efforts to come between them. "I'm glad you came clean, but interfering in my personal life, no matter what your intentions, was a deal breaker. I'll be looking for new friends."

Alex's face fell. Jason turned away from her, clutching his bag tightly, and made his way to the curb to hail a taxi. He felt justified in his words, but couldn't help notice a twinge of guilt at having spoken so harshly. Still, if he'd learned anything lately, it was that avoiding conflict wasn't the answer.

CHAPTER THIRTY-ONE

"I thought you might be avoiding me," Governor Carlton said, grinning. "After our meeting, I expected you to jump all over this project. I was surprised when you disappeared. But, Constance filled me in on your extenuating circumstances."

"The last few months have been a little bit challenging," Gwen said, smiling. The truth was, she had avoided thinking about the Governor's offer. He discussed all the details with her after the voter registration event, but since the work would not begin until November, she moved it to the back of the list of a million things she had to think about.

"The grant monies will be sent out in a few weeks, and I need to make sure we're ready to go when the funds arrive."

"Given my current ... situation, are you sure you want me to head up this task force?" Gwen didn't want a negative answer, but she felt compelled to ask. After all, she'd finally come to terms with the fact that being pregnant would have a big effect on her life and that the impact would be felt in her career.

The Governor chuckled, "When Constance was pregnant with our son, she sat on three boards and headed up the League of Women Voters. That was while I was in the legislature, and I certainly wasn't much help. That woman was so tired some days, she'd fall asleep while she ate dinner." Gwen cringed, but the Governor's expression was kind. "I never doubted for a second, and was confident she would succeed, despite trying to convince her to take it easy. And I don't doubt that you'll do whatever you set your mind to." He paused. "I guess the question is, do you still want the job?"

Gwen smiled. "Yes, I do."

She shook the Governor's hand, still in a bit of shock. When she'd gotten the call to come meet with Governor Carlton, she wasn't sure what to expect. In fact, she'd tried not to have any expectations. He was right, this task force was a chance to be involved in a cause in which she truly believed. As the head, she would be positioning herself well for state-level positions and other opportunities that might come along.

On her way back to Cambria, Gwen turned the radio up and sang along at the top of her lungs, on top of the world. When she got back to town, she pulled out her phone, ready to text Val the good news. Then it dawned on her that Val was still on her honeymoon. *I'm certainly not bothering her until she gets back,* Gwen chuckled, sure that Val was off having the time of her life. It was strange the ways their lives were beginning to diverge. As Val's relationship with John progressed, the cousins had found themselves with fewer chances to spend time together. It seemed the natural progression of life. Now Gwen would have a baby, and the world would change again.

She checked the time. It was too early to call Jason. So, she texted Victoria.

You busy?

What's up?

Just met with the Governor. Going to head up that task force.

That's great!!! So excited for you. Will call you tonight.

Gwen got back to her apartment. Jason had moved her desk into the living room, so she sat down and pulled out her laptop to work. She'd thought it would be strange working out in the open instead of her cozy office, but she found the ability to turn on the television for background noise more comforting than she'd expected.

Gwen worked on a report for one her clients, but her thoughts kept wandering. Things were coming together for her professionally, and she was grateful. But as she sat in her apartment, she felt strangely lonely. How would it be caring for a baby when Jason was on the road all the time? The whole Alex fiasco had really driven home the fact that Jason's travel could and probably would impact their relationship. As much as she loved him, she wondered if they could make it work.

CHAPTER THIRTY-TWO

Jason woke up Wednesday morning in a cold sweat. He was meeting with Bill Mackey today and after some careful consideration, he was pretty sure this might be his last week of work with BGB. Faced with the eventuality of losing a senior auditor in a few months, he assumed they would most likely want to cut their losses quickly. Jason would be distracted with finding a new job, and it was common for employees to slack off in their last days. Jason really couldn't blame Bill for being cautious, but the reality of losing his job without a backup sent Jason into a tailspin emotionally.

That's just great, he thought. *Your first big move as a father-to-be is to become gainfully unemployed right when your family needs you. Sweet move, idiot.*

Jason felt miserable. Truth was he really liked his work with BGB. It was more challenging than government work, and he didn't miss the drama of working at the city. He liked his co-workers and aside from his issues with Alex, things had been relatively smooth. He was proud of the work he'd done thus far, and he wasn't happy about leaving so soon.

The thing that kept Jason from changing his mind was an image that had cemented itself in his mind. In it, Gwen calls him to tell him that his child said her first word, *dada*, and Jason cries knowing he'd missed it. Jason had always been close to his parents, especially his father. Until they'd moved to Florida a few years ago, Jason and his father would hang out almost every weekend, watching sports at a pub or fishing. It had been very hard for Jason when his parents decided to move away. Regardless of his relationship with Gwen, Jason was determined to be the best father he could be. That required him being present.

Thoughts of the baby brought a smile to Jason's face, but soon enough he was trapped in his cycle of worry again. He wondered whether he'd find a job as satisfying as his position at BGB had been. He got ready to head to the office, full of anxiety about how the day would end.

At work, Jason was quickly absorbed in the day's tasks. He'd barely moved in an hour when his co-worker Phil stopped by his desk.

Jason pulled himself away from the spreadsheet he was studying. "Hi, Phil. How's it going?"

"Not bad. Almost done with the report you need. Just got a call from Bill Mackey. He's coming in today. I wondered if you knew what it's about. He wants to meet with me at one o'clock."

Jason sighed. This was it. Bill would give his job to Phil and Jason would be heading back to Cambria, tail between his legs. Jason debated spilling the beans to Phil but decided on restraint. He'd let the chips fall where they may.

"I'm meeting with him at two. I'll guess we'll find out," he said, vaguely, hoping to ward off any further questions.

"Hey, I wondered if you'd like to grab some lunch," Phil said, looking at his watch. "There's a great restaurant down the street, and we haven't had much opportunity to get to know each other yet." Phil looked hopeful.

"Sure. I should be done in about forty-five minutes. That work for you?"

"Perfect. I'll meet you out front."

Forty-five minutes later, Phil and Jason were walking down the street toward a Mexican restaurant Phil claimed served the best street tacos in town. They were seated near an ostentatious tiled fountain that sat at the center of the dining area. Exposed rafters overflowed with fake greenery, and plastic parrots were perched here and there. The gaudiness of the decor made Jason laugh.

Seeing Jason surveying his surroundings, Phil said, "I know. It's a little tacky, but I promise the food is amazing." He smiled.

"I believe you," Jason joked. "How long have you worked for BGB?"

"About three years. I moved into the western division about two years ago. Transferred from the east coast. My wife wanted to be closer to her family."

"Where do you live?"

"Denver. You're from Cambria right? That's a really nice town. We love the fall beer festival."

"Yep. Born and raised. I didn't realize you were from Denver. We should get together sometime."

Phil smiled. "You'll have to catch us soon. My wife's pregnant. She's due in a few weeks. Who knows what life will be like after that?" Phil paused for some chips and salsa. "It's our first kid. Everyone says to say goodbye to sleep."

"Congratulations! Actually, it's sort of lucky we hung out today. My girlfriend is pregnant too. I could use some advice. Or maybe a sympathetic ear."

"That's great! How far along is she?"

"About four months."

"Know what you're having yet? Or are you going to make it a surprise?"

Jason chuckled. "Gwen wants to know so she can decorate appropriately. She's not big on surprises. Actually, we have an ultrasound next week so hopefully we'll know soon."

"Jane wasn't about to wait either." He laughed. "We're having a little girl. Charlotte." Jason couldn't help but notice the twinkle in Phil's eye as he talked about his wife and child. It made Jason feel more at ease with his decision.

"I'm going to level with you, Phil. But please don't share this information. I spoke with Bill Mackey on Monday. I'm resigning." Seeing the look of shock on Phil's face, Jason explained. "I took the job before Gwen found out she was pregnant. I just want to be able to be there for my family."

Phil nodded. "I know how you feel." He paused, then added, "Do you have something else lined up?"

"No," Jason said, miserably. "I haven't even told Gwen yet. It seemed like a good idea on Monday but I think they might let me go today. Maybe I should have waited to talk to Bill. Anyway, I think they may offer you my job. Your work with the California audit was stellar."

Phil smiled. "Thanks. That means a lot." He took a sip of water. "At least we can be friends still. I'm glad we met up today."

"Me too. I've been so wrapped up in all my personal stuff, I haven't done much toward making friends at work. Now I wish I had."

"I thought you and Alex Barnes seemed pretty close." Phil averted his gaze, then, clearing his throat, he continued. "Actually, there's been some talk about you two being an item."

Jason frowned. "Really?"

"I probably shouldn't have said anything."

"Alex and I went to training together, and we hit it off right away, but she wants more than friendship. I didn't realize we'd become grist for the gossip mill. I can't believe how clueless I've been."

"You've had a lot on your mind." His expression softened. "Maybe we can get the girls together this weekend."

"That sounds great!" Jason said relieved by the change of subject.

Phil's words hit a nerve with Jason, and he was ruminating on them when, at a few minutes to two o'clock, he headed down the hall toward the conference room. He arrived to find Phil still sitting across from Bill Mackey.

"Sorry, I didn't mean to interrupt," Jason said, backing out the door.

Bill smiled. "No, no. Come on in and sit down."

Jason sat next to Phil. The two men fidgeted nervously under the enigmatic stare of their boss. Finally, Bill relaxed back into his chair.

"You two look like a couple of bulls lined up for the slaughter." Much to Jason's surprise, Bill laughed.

Jason felt himself relax.

"I have a proposition," Bill said. This was not going the way Jason had expected it to. "Jason, I hope you don't mind, but I told Phil about your plans to leave BGB." Jason nodded. "I needed a few days to think about how I wanted to proceed, and I think I've come up with a solution that will benefit everyone."

Jason looked at Phil, but Phil's expression was one of bewilderment. Clearly he had no idea what was coming, which made Jason wonder they'd been talking about earlier in their meeting.

Bill continued. "Phil, I know you've expressed some interest in cutting back the travel once your daughter is born. Jason finds himself in much the same situation. The bottom line is that you two are some of our best auditors, and I'm not fond of the idea of losing you both, but I can see that's where we're headed." Phil started to protest, but Bill held up a hand, his expression softening. "You don't need to defend yourself, Phil. You haven't come right out and asked, but once that baby is born, you're not going to want to be out of town all the time, and Jane's going to need your help."

Jason was touched that Bill had taken the time to get to know Phil's family situation. It reinforced his regret at leaving BGB.

"Here's my proposition. I have spots for two financial analysts in the Denver office. I spoke with corporate, and we've drawn up an offer for each of you. It won't be the same job you're doing now, but it'll be a lateral move, same pay, same benefits, and you'll only have to travel once or twice a year."

Bill grinned. Silence fell over the room. Jason was too shocked to speak, and a quick glance in Phil's direction told Jason he felt the same way. Jason had come to this meeting expecting to be let go. Phil hadn't expected any change at all. That Bill had gone out of his way to try and keep them both on board was a testament to his faith in them. Again, Jason felt touched, but he was still in too much shock to speak.

After a few moments, Bill said, "Don't thank me all at once." Then he laughed. "You've both transitioned to deer caught in headlights. I didn't realize I was so frightening. What's it going to be fellows? Because if the answer is yes, I'll need you both to do a lot of closing out and transitioning this week. I'd expect you to start in your new roles first thing Monday morning." He slid two folders across the table, one for Jason and one for Phil. "These are your new contracts. Job descriptions. Pay and benefit packages. Etcetera. Etcetera."

Jason opened up the folder and leafed through the papers. Finally, he looked at Bill and smiled. "You have no idea how much this means to me." He was surprised to find himself choking back emotion.

Bill smiled. "Oh, I think I do. I have four kids; my youngest just graduated high school. The time goes by fast, and I wouldn't trade a minute of it. BGB is a family company, despite its size, and my goal is to keep my employees happy so they'll work hard and stay with us."

Phil finally broke his silence. "I don't know what to say. I never expected this."

Bill chuckled. "Don't have a heart attack over there, Phil. I didn't create these jobs for you, but I'm happy I can offer them to you regardless. The timing was right." His expression returned to its usual sternness. "Now, if you agree to these terms, please sign your contracts, and then I'm going to brief you on what needs to get done this week."

An hour later, both men returned to their stations, ready for a few long days of closing out reports and transferring files to co-workers. Phil dialed his wife the minute they left the conference room, but Jason decided to wait. He had something a little more spectacular in mind.

CHAPTER THIRTY-THREE

Jason flew home late Friday night. Gwen told him briefly about her meeting with the Governor and her work on the task force. Jason had been really excited for her, but his energy was depleted. He'd told her about Alex's confession. At first, Gwen was angry but pretty soon her anger was replaced by pity. She'd snuggled in close to Jason and vowed never to take their relationship for granted again.

Val and John got back on Friday from their honeymoon. Gwen knew they'd need a few days to recover, but she'd still managed to talk Val into some coffee Saturday morning. Jason was still asleep. Gwen crept out of the apartment, hoping not to wake him. He'd worked late the last few nights, and each time he called Gwen, he sounded more exhausted.

When Gwen walked into Java Lite, a very sleepy-looking Val was already nursing a large coffee in the corner. Gwen got a cup of tea and joined Val.

"I'm starting to feel a little bad for getting you out this morning," Gwen teased, though she looked concerned.

Val laughed. "Don't look so shocked. I couldn't sleep on the plane on the way back, so I feel like a zombie." She took a big drink of coffee. "After this I intend to go back to bed, so it'll be okay."

"Was it everything you ever dreamed?"

Val's face became dreamy. "It was like a fairytale. Literally.

We visited these tiny little villages with buildings that dated back to the Middle Ages. It was breathtaking and kind of overwhelming."

"I want to hear every detail!" Gwen said, excitedly.

Val sighed. "Okay, but not today. I'm way too tired. What's new with you?"

"Jason moved in."

Val sputtered. "Really?"

"Yes, really," Gwen said, giggling. "A lot happened after your wedding. I told my mom off. I confronted Evan about stalking me. Jason moved in." Gwen paused, seeing that Val was overwhelmed with all this new information. "Oh, and that girl Jason works with, Alex, was the one sending all the flowers."

"You've got to be kidding," Val said, rolling her eyes. "What is she, sixteen? How'd you find out?"

"She confessed to Jason."

Val looked skeptical. "Wonder what made her do that?"

"Jason says she confessed having feelings for him, and he made it clear he didn't feel the same about her. Anyway, I honestly don't care anymore, and I'm ready to put it behind us. Things are going really well and I don't want to mess it up by letting my imagination run away with me. It's going to be hard enough with them continuing to work together."

Val smiled. "Good plan. Any news on the work front?"

"Big news," Gwen said, beaming. "I accepted the Governor's offer to head up that task force on violence against women and children. It'll mean more work, but I think it's going to be really rewarding."

Val leaned over to hug Gwen. "I'm so proud of you, Gwen. You're going to do so many great things in your life."

Gwen was startled to see Val getting teary. "Are you alright?"

"I'm fine," Val said, wiping away a tear and smiling. "I'm just so tired that I'm feeling weepy and sentimental. I'm truly happy for you and Jason. I was worried you wouldn't figure out how to stay together. Although I have no doubt that you are fully capable of taking care of yourself, it's nice to know you and the baby will have lots of help and love."

Gwen smiled, and patted Val's shoulder. "You kept telling me everything would be okay. I guess you were right."

Val yawned. "I think I'd better get going. I'm sorry to leave already, but I'm so exhausted I'm starting to feel ill. I think I need to go lie down."

Gwen grinned. "Wouldn't it be funny if you were pregnant?"

Val gave Gwen a crooked smile. "You're hilarious! I never knew pregnant women were so funny."

Gwen stood, helping Val to her feet. With a big hug, the two women said their goodbyes. Gwen made Val promise to text when she got home, concerned about how unsteady Val seemed to be on her feet. Secretly though, she was also relieved she was no longer the one who needed coddling.

Walking out into the crisp fall air, Gwen was overcome by a sense of calm. She'd endured some very chaotic months and was coming out the other side, strong and confident. She walked back to her car, relishing the crunch of the leaves beneath her boots. It was a few short weeks until Thanksgiving, and she was definitely feeling thankful.

CHAPTER THIRTY-FOUR

Gwen awoke from an afternoon nap, surprised to find flowers by her bedside. For a split second, she tensed, then she realized Jason was perched at the foot of the bed, smiling.

"Oh, boy," she said, sitting up slowly and grinning. "I'm going to have to get over my fear of flowers."

Jason chuckled. "I guess I shouldn't have done something so terrifying. It'll never happen again."

Gwen reached out her arms, and Jason moved up beside her on the bed. "By all means, please let it happen again." She kissed his cheek. "How long have you been sitting there?"

"Just a little while. I have a surprise."

"Oh?"

"But you have to get dressed up. I called John, and we're meeting them for dinner."

"I hope Val got some sleep. She looked like death this morning," Gwen said, hoping Val wasn't coming down with something. Being pregnant, the thought of even catching a cold was daunting given the restrictions on medications.

"John says she slept all day, so she should be okay. At least for a while."

"Maybe we can get some details about the honeymoon out of John. Val was too tired to talk much this morning." Gwen got up and stretched. "Where are we going?"

"I thought we'd try the new Brazilian grill downtown."

Gwen's stomach rumbled. "You certainly know the way to a girl's stomach." She patted her belly. "Baby approves of the choice, too."

Jason leaned down so his head was level with Gwen's belly. "You have excellent taste, baby. Can't wait to see you in person." The tender moment made tears well up in Gwen's eyes. She pulled Jason back up to standing, playfully.

"None of that. If I have to have a crying jag, we'll be late getting food, and I'm starving." She headed into the bathroom, then peeked her head back out. "Do I have time for a quick shower?"

"Yes, we're not due to meet them for an hour. I didn't want to rush you."

Gwen smiled. "Thanks, honey."

Half an hour later, Gwen walked into the living room, fidgeting with her dress.

"You look gorgeous," Jason said, smiling.

Gwen sighed. "I was going to wear pants, but they're all getting uncomfortable. It looks like I'll be wearing a lot of dresses until I have a chance to go shopping for some maternity pants."

"Shall we go?" Jason said, holding his arm out for Gwen.

"Please!" Gwen said, dramatically. "I'm going to pass out if I don't gorge on delicious roasted meat on a spit soon." She laughed all the way out to the car.

Gwen met her match in the Brazilian restaurant. At the end of dinner, she leaned back in her seat, too full to rest her arms on the table. Val and John stared at her with amused looks on their faces.

"I'm not sure where all that food went," John teased. "I think you ate more than I did."

Gwen gave John an indignant look, then smiled. "I'm eating for two, you know." She paused. "I guess I'm going to have to start watching what I'm eating or I'll be as big as an elephant."

Val smiled. "You look beautiful. After those first few months of hardly eating, I'm sure you need the extra calories." She looked rested, but Gwen still saw the dark circles her makeup wasn't quite hiding.

"We shouldn't keep you guys out too late," Gwen said, concerned.

Before Val responded, Jason jumped in. "Before we go our separate ways, I have some news. It's actually the reason I asked you guys to join us."

Val gave Gwen a questioning look, but Gwen shrugged. She had no idea what Jason meant.

"I quit my job," he announced.

"You what?" she said, her voice a little shrill, and she saw John shift uncomfortably in his seat.

Jason smiled. "Actually, I went to my boss on Monday and told him I wanted to resign before the baby comes so I wouldn't have to travel as much."

Gwen was in shock. Her temple throbbed and her hands felt a little clammy in her lap.

"Anyway," he said, sensing the need to speed things along before Gwen lost it. "He flew out to Arizona to meet, and I thought for sure he was going to let me go."

"Please tell me there's a *but* coming," Gwen said, still looking shaken.

"There's a but. Phil, he's a co-worker who lives in Denver whose wife is also pregnant, had apparently expressed similar wishes. So Bill, that's my boss, announces he's got two positions open at the Denver office for us." Jason smiled broadly. "I start on Monday. Same pay. Limited travel. No more hotel living."

The table was silent long enough to make Jason sweat. Then John said, "Congratulations!"

Gwen looked at Jason. "I'm shocked," she said, stating the obvious. "I'm happy but also a little shocked. You didn't tell me you were thinking of quitting your job."

Jason frowned. "Please don't be mad. I woke up Monday morning, and I packed my bag. It suddenly hit me that I was going to miss every special moment in my kid's life, and I detoured to the Denver office to talk to Bill."

Gwen smiled. "It'll be really nice having you at home. Commuting to Denver every day is going to get old, though."

Jason grinned. "Not as old as flying to a new city every week. If I never eat another peanut butter sandwich again, it'll be too soon."

Gwen laughed. "That was self-imposed torture, you know." She said, but she reached out to take his hand. "No, this is going to be great. I'm really happy." She leaned over to kiss him.

"That's good, because I have one more thing." Nervously, Jason got up and stood beside Gwen's chair. "Gwen, check your purse. I put something in there for safekeeping."

With a strange look on her face, Gwen reached down for her purse. She pulled out a big wad of newspaper. Handing it to Jason, she said, "What is that?" a suspicious look on her face, teetering dangerously close to disgust.

Jason laughed. "I'll show you." He began unwrapping the newspapers, and he got down on one knee.

A gasp from Val's direction caught Gwen's attention, and the color returned to her face. She turned back to face Jason and realized he now held a blue Tiffany ring box, having discarded the newspaper disguise.

"Gwendolyn Marsh. I know there are a lot of things going on in our lives right now, and before we get caught up in those other things, I want to ask you something." Jason cleared his throat. "I love you. Will you marry me? Please?" Before Gwen responded he said, "I bought this ring for you six months ago, so I assure this is not just about the baby. I admit, when you drove me crazy, I wondered if it would stay buried in my sock drawer forever. But I never doubted my love for you, and I'm so happy we didn't give up on each other." He winked. "After all, this is true love."

Tears were already spilling down Gwen's cheeks before she

croaked, "Yes." One little word, and then it was some time before Gwen got her emotions under control enough to say another word. When she glanced over at Val, she saw that Val was crying too. But John and Jason both looked panic-stricken, which made Gwen laugh.

She laughed so hard she had to excuse herself to the bathroom. When she returned to the table, Val finally stopped crying, and John had his arm about Val's shoulder, whispering into her ear.

Gwen sat down.

Jason said, "Now that you're back, I wondered if you'd like to try this ring on for size."

Gwen blushed. She'd been so busy crying and then laughing she'd forgotten all about the ring. She opened the box, took out the diamond solitaire, and handed it to Jason.

"Would you like to do the honors?" she said, grinning.

"Yes, ma'am." Jason slipped the ring on her finger.

Gwen marveled at the way the diamond sparkled under the restaurant lighting. Before she knew it, Val was on her feet and wrapped her arms around Gwen's neck.

Kissing Gwen's cheek, she said softly, "You look good in love, cousin."

* * *

Gwen and Jason's wedding was nothing like Val's. For all the time she'd spent imagining herself walking down the aisle, Gwen opted for an intimate wedding only a few weeks later with a few of their friends and family in attendance. It was simple and perfect.

After the ceremony, Jason and Gwen settled in for dinner with John and Val, Victoria and their new friends Phil and Jane. Phil looked nervously at Jane throughout the evening. Her due date had come and gone, and now everyday was possibly *the day*.

"How are you feeling, Jane?" Gwen asked across the table.

"Huge. Tired of being pregnant. Ready to meet this baby," Jane said, each word taking effort. "This is the most I've been out of the house in days. Poor Phil is going to have a heart attack if we don't have this baby soon." Jane grinned at her husband, squeezing his hand.

Gwen laughed. "Can't wait to see how Jason handles the pressure."

"I think surviving the wedding day is accomplishment enough. I need a few more months to work up to the delivery." Despite his mock indignation, Jason looked relaxed and happy.

Victoria raised her glass. "I'd like to toast Gwen and Jason on a beautiful wedding and the start of their lives together." Glasses clinked and smiles abounded as the friends talked about their lives. After a delicious dinner, cake was served. As everyone finished up their meals, Gwen and Jason stood.

Taking Jason's hand, Gwen said, "Thank you all for celebrating this day with us and for being part of this crazy journey." She smiled at Jason. "We went to the doctor yesterday, and found out we're having a girl."

The table erupted in applause. Jason pulled Gwen into his arms, kissing her passionately. Then he leaned in close to her ear and whispered, "Four more months."

Gwen smiled. "And then the fun really begins."

The *"Serious About Writing"* Publishing Package

Are you interested in publishing your fiction or non-fiction title with the prestige of an imprint? Do you want a staff of editors and designers to provide the best quality product possible? Is it important to keep your copyright and all profits from your book sales? Oh, and would you like it done in three months instead of the typical 18 months to two years required by a traditional publisher?

Look into our *"Serious About Writing"* package. We don't take commissions and don't give advances. We review your manuscript regardless if it's sent by you or by an agent. In exchange for an up-front one-time fee, we make sure your work is in the best shape possible and receives the acceptance it deserves.

Here are just some of the advantages:

- Expert editing and design staff.
- Personal service throughout all aspects of the process.
- Prestige of a third-party publisher.
- Distribution to Amazon, Kindle, and other outlets.
- Creation of ISBN & bar code.
- Retention of all copyrights.
- One hundred percent royalties.
- Completion and publication within 90 days.
- A marketing plan that can be implemented by the author.

You can choose multiple avenues to accomplish these same tasks, or take advantage of the *"Serious About Writing"* package. Contact us for more information at woodenpantspub@gmail.com. You can also visit our website, woodenpantspub.com, and fill out the form on the Publication page. We look forward to working with you toward your goal of author entrepreneurship!

CPSIA information can be obtained
at www.ICGtesting.com
Printed in the USA
LVOW01s1826060417
529886LV00008B/815/P